PRAISE FOR ROBERT J. CONLEY

"Powerful, often dealing with cruel events, yet imbued with a mystical aura, [Conley's] stories reflect the range of Cherokee culture and the differences among the full and mixed-blood inheritors."

—*Publishers Weekly*

"Robert Conley's *Mountain Windsong* deserves to become an American classic. Conley takes the grim facts of our 'Manifest Destiny' and makes them come alive in a novel which is beautiful and heartwarming as well as tragic."

— Tony Hillerman, *New York Times* bestselling author

"Clever plotting and an enigmatic protagonist guarantee a whole posse of happy readers."

—*ALA Booklist*

FUGITIVE'S TRAIL

"Robert Conley is one of the most inventive writers America has ever had . . . In Kid Parmlee, [Robert Conley] has created a second-hand Billy the Kid who will charm your damned ears off and send you down a trail of fun, frivolity, and adventure. Go buy it right now, read it and enjoy it."

—Max Evans, author of
The Rounders, The Hi-Lo Country, and *Bluefeather Fellini*

More . . .

"[Conley is] versatile: poetry, humor, historical Western, mystery, even horror. Now, Kid Parmlee. Neither a traditional general Western character, [nor] a super-hero of anti-hero caricature, he is simply Kid Parmlee, a human being. In his pathetic way, Kid Parmlee is not a very good person, but also only as bad as survival requires. Simply clever, good and bad, sad and funny, failure and success . . . 'The Kid' holds up a mirror to the human condition."

—Don Coldsmith, author of
the Spanish Bit Series and *Bearer of the Pipe*

"Kid Parmlee ain't much shucks with the King's English, but he's loud and clear when he talks with his six-shooter."

—Elmer Kelton

"Conley's newest Western . . . [has] wit and a plot that bounces from one trouble-brewing scene to the next. Simple yet charming prose . . . ."

—*Publishers Weekly*

NED CHRISTIE'S WAR

ROBERT J. CONLEY

St. Martin's Paperbacks

NED CHRISTIE'S WAR

ISBN: 0-312-98487-1

Printed in the United States of America

Previously published by M. Evans & Company, Inc.
Pocket Books edition / September 1993
St. Martin's Paperbacks edition / August 2002

St. Martin's Paperbacks are published by St. Martin's Press, 175 Fifth Avenue, New York, NY 10010.

10 9 8 7 6 5 4 3 2 1

Prologue

No one knows just how old the game is: *digada-yosdi*. Marbles, they call it when they're talking English, or sometimes five hole. It may be as old as the Cherokees themselves, or they might have learned it from the white men and modified it to their own tastes. For the Cherokee game of marbles is not the marbles that white men know. The marbles are stones about the size of billiard balls, painstakingly polished into near-perfect spheres. The game has some of the characteristics of billiards, some of golf, some of horseshoe pitching, and some of croquet. The playing field is anywhere from 105 to 120 feet long, with holes in the ground every 35 to 40 feet. The first four holes are laid out in a straight line. Hole number five is set off at a right angle from number four, so that the entire line-up of holes forms an *L* shape.

The game is played by two teams, and it has a simple object. In order to win, each member of one team must get his marble into each hole. When the fifth hole is successfully achieved, the players turn back and go through the first four holes again, in reverse order. It is, therefore, a nine-hole game. To complicate the game, there are ways for a player to knock his opponent's marble out of the way, and it is possible for one member of a team to set up delaying tactics at one hole, holding back the opposing team while his own team members move ahead. It's a game requiring both skill and strategy, and Ned Christie was famous locally for both.

Ned had been at number eight for a long while. It was not that he was unable to reach nine. He had been holding there purposely to thwart the efforts of the opposing team. He had knocked three of their balls out of the way and allowed the other four members of his own team to reach the ninth hole. He was waiting for his next turn when Bearpaw, one of his opponents, made a vigorous toss toward number nine. The ball came to rest inches from the hole. There were still two other members of Bearpaw's team with Ned at number eight, but it was Ned's turn to play.

He picked up his marble and turned to face the final hole. He could try for the hole, or he could aim at Bearpaw's marble to try to knock it out of play. The marble was by far the easier target, and everyone expected Ned to hit it. The other players, those of Ned's team who had already finished and those of Bearpaw's who were waiting for their turn, all stopped joking, chatting, and milling around to watch Ned's play. Ned leaned slightly forward, holding the ball in both hands in front of himself. He stared straight ahead. Then suddenly he drew back his right arm and made a sharp, underhand toss. The marble zipped the thirty feet or so through the air and rammed itself into the hole. It was an amazing toss, even for Ned.

Victory shouts came from the mouths of Ned's teammates and groans from the losers, all the talk, of course, in Cherokee. There was no English spoken here.

"Ah," shouted Bearpaw, "he's done it again."

A woman's voice rose shrilly above all this good-natured banter. "Come and eat," she called.

"We'd better go," said Ned.

He led the way from the playing yard over to the front of the cabin, where the women were gathered at the fires. Boards had been laid across upended logs to make a temporary table and benches, where food was displayed. The men went to the tables, sat down, and helped themselves; only when the men had taken all they wanted did the women sit down on the other side of the table and call the children.

"Come on, little ones."

The children rushed at the table like a flock of chickadees going after spilled seed. But when they reached the table, they stopped. They stood at the table or found seats where they could between the women, who served them their meals. It was a veritable feast. There was corn bread and bean bread. There were grape dumplings. There was venison and squirrel and gravy, and there was a wide variety of wild greens. It was a festive occasion for no particular reason, and everyone was having a fine time. Then Bearpaw injected a little seriousness into the air.

"There's a council meeting tomorrow?" he asked.

"Not tomorrow," said Ned. "The next day. Tomorrow I'll ride to Tahlequah."

"Of course," said Bearpaw. "That's what I meant to say. What will you talk about at the meeting?"

"What the railroad has done to us?" asked Peeks Above.

"There are too many white people in the Cherokee Nation," said Bearpaw.

"The real problem," said Ned, "is that too many of those whites can vote. If they're married to Cherokees, we give them citizenship. Then they can vote. And they vote for mixed-bloods who are more like them than they are like us."

"Pretty soon," said Bearpaw, "we'll have a council of white people."

"It's getting like that already," said Ned. He stood up and tossed a squirrel bone toward one of the dogs. Then he turned and walked into the house.

"There are people who want to make this another state," said Bearpaw. "They want to do away with our government and with our tribal lands. They want to make us just like white people. Give each of us our own little private farms. Allotment, they call it. I've heard they're already doing it to other Indians. There won't be any more Cherokee Nation. There won't be any more Cherokees."

Peeks Above had just taken a big bite of bean

bread. He looked up at Bearpaw for an instant. Then he dropped his eyes back down to the table.

"No," he said. "Ned Christie won't let them do that."

Chapter 1

Maletha Maples was worried, but she kept her thoughts to herself. She almost always did. It was not an easy life, being the wife of a deputy United States marshal and a mother of six children. Every time Dan rode out on an assignment, she wondered if she would see him again. It was widely known that more than sixty of Judge Parker's deputies had been killed in the Indian Territory in the line of duty. But it didn't pay for a woman to complain. And Dan did make a good living. She liked their little house in Bentonville, Arkansas, with its neat yard and white picket fence. She liked being known and respected in the community, and she knew, of course, that it was all due to Dan and his job.

But when Sam had asked if he could ride along this time, and Dan had said okay, Maletha had protested. It would be too dangerous, she had said, and Sam was just a boy.

"I'm sixteen," Sam had said, a stubborn pout on his face.

"He's just about grown," said Dan. "Besides, it's just a routine assignment, Maletha. I'm going to look for Bill Pigeon. He's not a dangerous fugitive."

"He's wanted for murder," said Maletha.

"That's true," said Dan, "but he's never used violence to resist arrest. He's not considered dangerous. And George Jefferson and Mack Peel will be along. And a cook. That's five of us altogether."

"That's five counting Sam," Maletha had said, and Dan had given her a stern look, a look that meant that he had made up his mind.

"That's five," he had said, "counting Sam. He's going to be grown soon. I need to spend more time with him."

So Maletha had said no more. She went about her business with a lined, long face that morning. She fed her husband and all six children. She laid out the clothes for Dan and Sam to pack. And she kept her lips clamped tight. The smaller children raced around the house as usual, shouted and cried and picked at each other as usual. And all too soon, for Maletha, it was over and done.

"We'll be on our way," said Dan. Sam was right behind him. They stood on the porch while Maletha and the five younger children came out behind them. Dan hugged and kissed each child in its turn, and Sam, feeling very big, did the same. Maletha stifled an impulse to stand stern and haughty. Instead she put her arms around her husband and held him tight.

"Be careful," she said, "and take care of Sam."

"Aw, Mom," said Sam. "I can take care of myself. Don't worry."

Dan Maples smiled and looked down into the lined face of his wife.

"That's right," he said. "Don't worry."

He broke loose from her embrace and walked down the stairs and out to the gate. Just as his hand touched the latch on the gate, there was a sudden loud fluttering, and a large crow dropped from the sky and perched on his shoulder. Dan shouted in spite of himself, and Maletha shrieked. Dan slapped at the black, feathered intruder. It cawed and flew away. Maletha had turned ghostly pale.

"It's a sign," she said.

Dan stared at her in silence for a moment.

"Maletha," he said.

"It's a bad sign. Dan, don't go. Don't go this time."

"Maletha," he said. "It was just a bird."

"Just this one time. For me. Don't go."

But he did go, and so did Sam. They met Jefferson and Peel and the young cook, whom they all refused to call by any name but Cookie. They took a pack horse and a tent and camp supplies and food, and they left Bentonville heading west for Tahlequah. And Sam thought that he could see something in his father's face, something dark. In spite of what Dan had said to Maletha, riding along the trail west, he seemed to be deeply troubled, distraught, preoccupied with thoughts of something sinister. And Sam

thought about the crow, and he thought about his
mother's words.

Ned Christie was up early. Gatey was up, too. She
went over to the front of the cabin to build up her
fire. The weather was still warm, and they had slept
outside that night. Arch was sleeping, one old hound
sprawled out beside his head. Ned walked down to
the creek and knelt. He leaned over and bathed his
face and hands in the cold, clean water. He stood up
and walked back toward the house. On his way he
slowed enough to give Arch a kick in the rump with
the side of his foot.

"Hey," he said. "Wake up. You'll miss the day."

Arch sat up, his eyes bleary, and looked around.

When Ned reached the cabin, Gatey handed him
a cup of coffee. It was steaming, and Ned took a
tentative slurp.

"Ah," he said. "It's good."

"Your clothes are laid out for you inside on the
bed," said Gatey.

"Wado," Ned thanked her. "I'll pack them up after I eat."

His mind was already in Tahlequah. *Talikwa.* The
national capital. The capital city of the Cherokee Nation. There would be excitement in Tahlequah. There
always was when the council was in session. People
would come from all over the Cherokee Nation to
find out firsthand what new laws their council might
enact, to present their petitions, to air their com-
plaints and grievances. They would go to Tahlequah
simply because others were going. They went to see

friends they only saw in Tahlequah when the council was in session. But they also went to Tahlequah because they knew that the council would be dealing with important issues, issues that would directly affect their daily lives. Though the United States of America was much larger than the Cherokee Nation, a meeting of the bicameral Cherokee National Council was exactly analagous to a session of the United States Congress.

Ned Christie was acutely aware of that. He was keenly, at times almost painfully, conscious of the burden he carried as an elected representative of the people of his district. No living Cherokee could recall when times had not been hard, but in Ned Christie's mind, the Cherokees were on the brink of what might easily become the worst crisis in their long and troubled history. They had survived wars with the United States in the early days, they had lost land treaty by treaty until they had finally been subjected to the terms of the fraudulent Treaty of New Echota in 1835. That one had resulted in the loss of all their ancestral lands in the East. They had been forced west to new lands. To get to them, they had endured the Trail of Tears along which thousands had died. They had built a new nation in the West and established their capital at Tahlequah. But there had been a bitter division among the Cherokees over the signing of that treaty, and much bloodshed had resulted. A brief period of peace and prosperity had followed. Then came the white man's Civil War, and once again the Cherokees had split apart. The Civil War left many dead, and it left the Cherokee Nation a desolate heap of ashes. And it had given the United States an excuse to take away more Cherokee land. The Cherokee Nation had been made to suffer more at the hands of the United States after the Civil War than had any of the seceding southern states.

And now, just fifty-two years later—less than one man's lifetime—since the Treaty of New Echota, which promised to leave Cherokee lands alone forever, the sovereignty of the Cherokee Nation was once again being threatened by the powerful United States. They said the Cherokee Nation had no jurisdiction over whites, and whites were everywhere in the Cherokee Nation. Many of them were lawbreakers. Then they said the Cherokees could not maintain law and order. How could they, when the United States would not let them? But they used that as an excuse to establish the federal court at Fort Smith and to give it jurisdiction over what they called the Indian Territory. That included the Cherokee Nation, the Creek Nation, the Chickasaw Nation, the Choctaw Nation, and the Seminole Nation. They lumped them together and called them Indian Territory. Ned despised the term.

So now the threat had become the total dissolution of the Cherokee Nation, and the creation of a new state that would be made of Indian Territory and the territory further west called Oklahoma. There would be no more tribal land. Each Cherokee would be made a private landowner just like the whites. Private ownership of land was a concept foreign to Cherokees and repugnant to the Cherokee worldview.

It was a hard time to be a councilor, a time of great danger and a time of tremendous responsibility for public servants. Ned knew all these things, and he felt that responsibility. All of this was in his mind as he prepared himself for the trip to Tahlequah. Bitterness over the past, desperation about the present, and cautious, anxious hope for the future drove him in his perceived duty, a duty he owed to all Cherokees, living, dead, and yet to come.

He rolled his clean clothes in a blanket and tied the blanket roll with leather thongs. Outside, Arch had saddled his gray mare and had it waiting. Ned tied the roll behind the saddle.

Tahlequah was just as he had anticipated, as he had seen it before when the council had been in session. Riding into town he saw several people he knew. They waved and shouted greetings. He stopped in front of the National Hotel and hitched his mare to the rail. Taking the blanket roll, he went inside and registered for a room. He took the key, walked to the room, and unlocked the door. He tossed the blanket roll onto the bed, glanced around the room, and left. He wouldn't need the room until later, but soon there would be no more rooms available. That was the main reason for his early arrival in town. He was established for the duration of his stay in Tahlequah, and it was only a little after noon. The meeting was scheduled for the next morning. He decided to stroll around the town to see whom he could see, but first he would take the mare to the stable at the other end of town.

The main street was crowded with wagons, buggies, riders on horseback, and pedestrians. Making his way through the tangle, Ned saw other acquaintances. They waved or spoke greetings. Some spoke in Cherokee, others in English. At home with his family and neighbors, Ned spoke almost exclusively Cherokee, but when he came to Tahlequah, he had to be prepared to speak in either language and to switch back and forth when the circumstances called for it. He spoke both languages well, and that fact gave him a certain amount of pride. It made him a much more effective councilor, too. He was sure of that.

The man at the livery stable spoke only English, though he was a Cherokee citizen, a mixed-blood. Ned knew him from other times when he had come to town. He talked with the man briefly, left his horse, and started walking back toward the hotel, walking over the same area he had just ridden. He walked on the board sidewalk, and he had to step aside when two small boys, perhaps ten or eleven years old, came running hard from the other direction.

"Hey," he said, as they swept past him, "where's the fire?"

He spoke in English because one of the boys was blond. As he turned back to continue his walk, a man stood in front of him.

" '*Siyo, Nede,*" said the man.

" '*Siyo, Doi,*" said Ned, and he continued to speak in Cherokee. "I haven't seen you for a long time."

"Not since the last council meeting," said *Doi*.

"That's right. You live a long ways from here."

"Pretty far. Yes," said *Doi*. "But I get here for the meetings. I don't want you councilors to do something I don't know about."

Doi laughed at his own joke, and Ned laughed with him.

"Where are you going?" said *Doi*.

"Just walking," said Ned. "I don't have anything to do until morning. I come early so I can get a room."

"Tahlequah fills up fast," said *Doi*. "I'll walk along with you."

They continued walking north, back toward the hotel Ned had checked into, and they talked as they strolled along. Now and then someone spoke to one or the other or both of them. There was a holiday atmosphere in Tahlequah, and in spite of himself, Ned began to feel it. He knew that the meeting in the morning would put him back in the mood he needed to be in, so he didn't let it worry him much. But he didn't have to wait. *Doi* suddenly became serious.

"I've heard some bad talk," he said.

"What kind of bad talk?"

"They say the white people want to take over all of our land here. They want another state. Like Arkansas and Texas. Is that true?"

"I've heard that talk," said Ned.

"What do they want with another state? They already have lots of states."

"They always want more," said Ned. "For a white man there is never enough."

"But can they do it?"

Ned looked grim.

"If they decide to do it," he said, "they can do it. But I think that they'll try to do it legally, and that means that we have to vote on it. If we vote no, they won't do it. If we vote yes, they will."

Doi laughed. "Why would we vote yes to give up our own country?"

"We wouldn't," said Ned. "You and me. But we have lots of mixed-blood citizens. Some of them are almost white. They think like the whites. They might want to have a state and be like the white people. We get more of them on the council each election. It could happen if we don't work hard against it."

They walked on in silence until they came to the center of town. Ned stopped. Directly across the street from them was the national capitol building. An imposing, two-story brick structure, its presence dominated the small town. Ned looked at the building with mixed feelings. It was not yet fifteen years old. It was a source of pride, and yet just looking at it caused the bitterness to well up from deep inside him. Had the Cherokee Nation erected this fine capitol just for the white man to steal?

"I'm going over there," he said.

"Well," said *Doi*, "I'll see you later. I'm going back to my camp. My wife will be wondering about me."

Ned dodged traffic to get across the street. The capitol stood in the middle of a large square, and in the square were a number of stately old trees. Benches were placed here and there beneath the trees. He walked slowly toward the front door of the building, looking up, feeling pride, feeling resentment at the forces that would take all this away from the Cherokees.

"Ned Christie," someone said.

Ned turned and looked toward the sound. A man was sitting on a bench under a shade tree. When Ned saw him, the man smiled and raised a hand.

"Ha," said Ned. "John Parris. It's good to see you again."

Ned was speaking English this time. Parris was a mixed-blood who did not speak Cherokee. Ned walked over and sat on the bench beside him.

"You're here for the meeting?" said Parris.

"Of course," said Ned. "I have to be here."

Parris snorted.

"It's all wasted energy, Ned," he said. "This Cherokee Nation is doomed. The United States has gone from the east coast to the west coast. It's north of us and it's south of us. They're not going to let us stay here. This is going to be the next state. Right here. You wait and see."

"Maybe you're right," said Ned. "But I'm going to fight it."

"John Ross fought to keep us in the east," said Parris. "Look where we are now. Hey. You want a drink? I'll buy it."

Ned thought about John Ross and the Trail of Tears, and he thought about the beautiful capitol building and about statehood.

"Where do you get it?" he said.

Liquor was absolutely forbidden in the Cherokee Nation, but it was widely known that it was also readily available if one knew the source. Parris gestured with his thumb over his shoulder toward the north end of town.

"Jennie Shell sells good whiskey down at her house," he said. "What do you say?"

"Okay," said Ned. "Let's go."

Chapter 2

Jennie Shell opened the door of her house on the north end of Tahlequah's main street cautiously. Her face wore a look of suspicion, but when she recognized John Parris, she smiled.

" 'Siyo, John," she said. She looked at Ned. "Is he with you?"

"Yeah," said Parris. "Ned's with me. You got a bottle of whiskey?"

"You got the price?" said Jennie.

"Is it the same as before?"

"Same as always," said Jennie.

"I got it. I got it right here," said Parris, and he stuffed his left hand into a pants pocket.

"Wait," said Jennie, glancing furtively toward town. "Go around to the north window. You know."

"Oh, yeah," said Parris. "Come on, Ned."

Jennie shut and latched the door, and Parris walked around to the north side of the little house. Ned followed. They waited there beside a window,

masked from anyone in town who might be looking
in that direction. Then Jennie opened the window
from inside, and, holding a bottle in one hand, stuck
out the other palm up. Parris dropped some cash into
it, and Jennie looked it over carefully, counting. She
handed the bottle out to Parris and shut the window.
Parris pulled out the cork and took a quick swig,
then passed the bottle to Ned. Ned took a drink and
felt the whiskey burn its way to his guts. He gave
the bottle back to Parris.

"Let's get away from here," he said.

They crossed to the west side of the road, looking
nervously south, toward town, and went into hiding
in the woods. They had gone only a few steps into
the shadows when Parris tipped the bottle again.

"Here," he said. Ned took the bottle and had another swallow. It burned only a little less than had
the first one. But it made him uneasy. He was, after
all, an elected official, a lawmaker, and the law of
his nation forbade liquor of all kinds. Not only that,
his religion, also, taught him that the white man's
spirit water was no good for Cherokees. Yet just this
time, he wanted it. The pressures were too many.
The United States government was a big and powerful adversary. It was enemy enough alone, but
there were forces within his own nation working
against what he knew to be the best interests of the
Cherokees. Well, he would get drunk on John Parris's *wisgi* tonight. Perhaps it would help. He would
forget everything for a few hours. Relax. In the
morning he would again be sober and serious. But
he couldn't afford to be seen. Not drunk. Not drink-

ing. Not with John Parris and his *wisgi*.

"Come on," he said, and he led Parris farther into the woods. He stopped at last at a spot where a small space was clear. It was like a room in the woods, and he felt safe.

"This is good," he said. He took a third swig from the bottle and passed it to Parris. Parris took a big gulp and sat down heavily on the ground, leaning back against a tree. Ned stayed on his feet. He took the bottle again and drank again, and he began to feel his head getting lighter. He also felt a sudden need to give words to the bitter and angry feelings he had stored inside. He turned angrily on Parris, so suddenly that Parris was startled.

"You know what they're trying to do?" he asked.

"Who?"

"Allotment. Statehood. They want all our land, and they want us to become white men. Or die. Or disappear. That's what they want."

He noticed that his speech was becoming slightly slurred. His tongue felt a little thick and slow. He squatted on his haunches there in front of Parris, and he put his hands heavily on Parris's shoulders and looked him straight in the eyes for a brief moment.

"John," he said, "you know we don't believe in owning land. All Cherokees own all the land. A man can't own the land. It's wrong."

"Times change," said Parris. He started to take a drink, but Ned took the bottle out of his hands and stood up with it. Ned took another drink.

"Some things never change," he said. "There's right and there's wrong."

"Give me a drink," said Parris.

Ned looked around.

"Oh," he said. He handed. Parris the bottle, and he started to pace nervously about in the small clearing.

Parris had not moved. He sat leaning against the tree. Once again, Ned had the bottle. He held it by the neck with his right hand as he still paced back and forth. His manner was agitated, his movements quick yet unstable, his gestures wildly, jerkily animated. He was speaking in Cherokee. Parris made a valiant attempt to raise up his head to look at Ned.

"You know," he said, "that I can't understand a goddamned word you're saying, don't you?"

If Ned heard, he paid no attention. He continued stumbling around and delivering his angry speech. Then he stopped, stood weaving on rubbery legs, and took another drink. The bottle was almost empty. He held it up in front of his eyes and studied it for a moment. Then he turned to look at Parris, sitting there on the ground. He stretched out his arm, offering the bottle to Parris. Parris lifted a weak arm and waved it away.

"I'm drunk," he said.

Ned staggered and dropped to his knees. He tipped up the bottle and finished the whiskey, then dropped the bottle and fell forward, catching himself with his hands. He crawled on hands and knees a few feet toward Parris, then let himself down to the ground. He mumbled something that Parris could not understand, and he buried his face in his arms and relaxed. Parris stared at him for a long moment. Ned didn't move. Parris struggled to his feet and stumbled the short distance to where Ned lay. He bent over and touched Ned on the shoulder. Ned didn't move. He gave Ned a tentative nudge. There was no reaction. He straightened himself up, shrugged, turned, and staggered off through the woods.

The morning the meeting was scheduled to begin, Dan Maples led his small posse up to the creek just north of Tahlequah. As he sat on his horse looking toward town, he saw Jennie Shell's house across the creek and to his left. Not far to his right a little footbridge crossed the creek.

"This will be good right here," he said, and he swung down out of the saddle. He felt stiff and sore from the long ride. A walk would help get the kinks out. He looked back over his shoulder toward the others.

"George," he said, "let's you and me go on down into town while the others set up camp."

"Okay, Dan," said Jefferson.

"You boys take care of the horses," said Maples, "set up the tents, build a fire. Cookie, some hot coffee would taste real good about the time we get back."

"Yes, sir," said Cookie.

"We're going on down," Maples continued, "ask a few questions, nose around a bit."

"Mr. Maples," said Cookie. "We could use a slab of bacon. If you want some."

"Anything else?"

"Eggs?" said Mack Peel.

"We'll see what we can do," said Maples. "Come on, George."

Maples and Jefferson walked toward the foot-bridge while the others got busy with their assignments. Maples led the way. The bridge was just a couple of logs laid across the creek and stabilized on either end with large rocks piled on each side. Jefferson followed Maples across the bridge, then caught up and walked along beside him.

"That's Jennie Shell's house, ain't it?" said Jefferson.

"Yeah," said Maples. "We'll stop and see her on the way back."

They walked on down the road and into town, careful to avoid the heavy traffic.

"What's going on here?" said Jefferson.

"I think they're having a big council meeting to-day," said Maples. "That draws them in from all over the Nation."

"Oh."

A Cherokee man stood with his arms folded, lean-ing against a storefront, watching the activity around him. He saw Maples approaching and grinned.

"Hello, Dan," he said.

"Hello, there, Jackson," said Maples. He walked on up to the man and stopped. Jefferson stopped be-side him. "Do you all know each other?"

"No," said Jefferson, "I don't believe so."

"Jackson," said Maples, "this is George Jefferson. He's a deputy marshal working with me out of Fort Smith. George, this here is Jackson Gourd. He's a captain of the Cherokee Light Horse Police here in Tahlequah."

Jefferson and Gourd shook hands.

"What brings you all to Tahlequah?" asked Gourd.

"Aw," said Maples, "they gave me the warrant on ol' Bill Pigeon. We're out here to try to serve it. Is there any way you can help us out?"

"Far as I know," said Gourd, "Bill just hangs out around home. You know where he lives, don't you?"

"Yeah. I know."

"Well, that's all I can tell you. I ain't seen him around here."

"Others have gone out to his house," said Maples, "and they always come back empty-handed. They say no one's home. They can't find him."

"You know what they say 'bout that 'round here, don't you?" said Gourd.

"Magic?" said Maples, a slight sneer on his face, but he thought about the crow, and the thought irritated him.

"Medicine," corrected Gourd. "Cherokee medicine. He's out there watching you guys."

"Sure," said Maples. "Sitting up on a tree branch in an owl's skin. I don't buy that. It's all bullshit."

"Well," said Gourd with a shrug, "go on out there and get him then. You know I can't help you none. Jurisdiction problems. Your law, not mine."

"I know," said Maples. "Is there anyone else in town I could talk to who might be able to help me out?"

"Lots of folks in town, Dan, but anyone you talk

to who knows ol' Bill will likely tell you just what I did. Good luck."

"Yeah. Thanks," said Maples. "Let's go, George."

"Nice meeting you, Jackson," said George.

"Yeah," said Jackson. "Same here."

They walked on down the sidewalk for a ways before Jefferson finally spoke.

"Sitting on a tree branch?" he asked.

"He was right about one thing," said Maples.

"What's that?"

"Anyone we talk to, we'll get that same story."

Ned Christie opened his eyes. He rolled over on his back with a groan. For a moment he wondered where he was. Then he remembered. He lolled his head over to the right, and he saw the empty bottle there on the ground. He groaned again, and he became conscious of a dull pain just between his eyes. Then he twisted his head to the left. He saw the big tree John Parris had sat under, but Parris was nowhere to be seen. He let his neck relax, and his head rolled back to a more comfortable position. His eyelids closed again. He should probably sleep a little longer.

Maples and Jefferson questioned a few more people, but they didn't get any useful information about Bill Pigeon. Maples hadn't really expected to. He knew that the Cherokees considered the federal law to be an intruder into their own jurisdiction, and in a way, he guessed he couldn't blame them. None of them, including their own police, had any real desire to help the U.S. marshals. And that feeling was even stronger, if that were possible, with this Bill Pigeon case. Pigeon was a popular man with the Cherokees. Well-known and well-liked, he was considered by many to be the most powerful medicine man the Cherokees had. Indian doctor, the Cherokees called it. Well, thought Maples, they would just have to ride out there to Bill Pigeon's house like the others had done before. They, too, would probably find it empty, and the Cherokees would all laugh and say that Bill Pigeon had been there, invisible or some such thing, watching their every move. He had the feeling that people around town were laughing at him already. Try to catch Bill Pigeon? Ha! Well, by God, he would try.

He pointed out a store to Jefferson, and they went inside and bought the bacon and eggs. Jefferson bought himself a five-cent cigar and tucked it into a shirt pocket for later use. Maples paid for the eggs and bacon but let Jefferson tote the package. They headed back toward their camp. Along the way they stopped and talked to a few more people, none for very long, none to any useful purpose. If anyone who knew anything was willing to talk, they had not found that person. When they had just about reached the creek, Maples angled over toward Jennie Shell's house. Jefferson followed. Jennie saw them coming and stepped out the front door to await their arrival. She stood, hands on hips, a scowl on her face.

"What do you laws want with me?" she said.

"Now, Jennie," said Maples, "don't get all upset. We just want to ask you a few questions."

"Questions about what?"

"Bill Pigeon," said Maples.

"I don't know him."

"Surely you've heard of him," said Maples.

"No, I ain't."

"Oh, come on. He's the most famous Indian doctor in these parts. Everyone knows him."

"I don't. Now I got things to do."

She turned her back on the deputies as if to go back into her house, but the sudden sharp tone in Maples's voice stopped her.

"Jennie," he said, "you know I carry whiskey warrants with me, don't you? You know what a whiskey warrant is?"

"I know," said Jennie.

"You know I could go into your house and look around, and if I was to find something that shouldn't be there, I could just write your name in that blank space on that whiskey warrant, and I could take you back with me to Fort Smith. You know that?"

"I don't know what you're talking about," she said. "Why you want to pick on me? A woman all alone. I don't know nothing about Bill Pigeon."

Jefferson shifted the package of eggs and bacon to his other arm, and Maples exhaled a loud sigh.

"All right," he said. "But we'll be watching your north window. Come on, George."

They walked back to the footbridge, and Jefferson, anxious to put down his burden, stepped up on the logs ahead of Maples. They could see the smoke rising from Cookie's fire, and they could smell the coffee. Jefferson was about halfway across. Maples was a few steps behind him. Back in the woods on the south side of the creek, to the rear of the deputies, a man stepped out from behind a tree. He stood in the shadows as he raised his right arm and pointed a revolver. His thumb pulled back the hammer until it clicked twice.

Sam Maples was squatted beside the fire when the first shot rang out. He looked toward the creek and saw Jefferson running, dropping his package into the creek as he ran for the north creek bank. He saw his father pull out his revolver and then jerk as the second shot sounded. He watched as his father fell into the creek, and he heard three more shots fired. He screamed as he came to his feet and ran toward his father, who was just there in the water, who was not moving anymore.

Chapter 3

Sam splashed into the creek where Maples was lying face down in the cold, clear water. His hand no longer gripped the revolver he had drawn. It was a few feet away under the water on the rocks—unfired. Sam grabbed at Maples and rolled him over. He reached under the dangling arms and gripped him around the chest, hugging him desperately to his own breast, sobbing, calling to him over and over, hoping for an answer from his father's lips. Cookie waded into the creek and picked up Maples's feet.

"Come on, Sam," he said. "Let's get him out of here."

George Jefferson and Mack Peel stood at the north end of the footbridge, guns in hands, crouched, bobbing one way and then the other, looking across the creek toward the trees on the other side. They could find no target. The mysterious gunman was gone.

"He must have run on back in the woods," said Peel.

"Come on," said Jefferson. "Let's find the son of a bitch."

Jefferson was again about halfway across the bridge. This time it was Sam Maples who stopped him.

"George," shouted Sam, the desperation clear in his voice. "Help us. What are we going to do?"

Jefferson paused, looked uncertain for a moment, then ran back to where Sam and Cookie sat with the unconscious Maples.

"Someone's coming from town," said Mack Peel.

Jefferson looked up. He recognized Jackson Gourd.

"That's the local police," he said.

Gourd, a few others behind him, came running into the deputies' camp. He saw at once what had happened.

"Dan?" he said.

"Someone shot him," said Sam.

"Come on," said Gourd. "Let's get him into town. We'll take him to Doc Blake's. Come on."

Back in the woods a mysterious figure ran through the shadows, and not far away, Ned Christie once more came awake. This time he sat up. He rubbed his eyes. He looked through the canopy of branches and leaves toward the sky, trying to figure out how far into the morning he had slept, but he couldn't tell. He stood slowly up on his feet and took a deep breath. Yes. He was all right. He was all right, but he was a mess, and he had the council meeting to attend. He felt in his pocket and found the key to the hotel room. He would go to the room, clean up and change his clothes. Then he would go to the capitol building and the meeting. For the remainder of his stay in Tahlequah, it would be all business.

Sam Maples stood with his back to the wall in a room in a strange building in Tahlequah. He was farther away from home than he had ever been before. Against the opposite wall in the small room was the bed where they had laid his father. Dan Maples was alive but unconscious. He had not said a word since the first shot had hit him. He was alive, but there was so much blood. Sam looked as if he had lost all his own blood, although, of course, he had lost none. He was deathly pale from fear and worry, and he felt squeamish, weak, lightheaded, dizzy, and, yes, even faint from watching the doctor, a stranger to Sam, hover over his father and fuss over the bullet wounds. Sam wondered if the man knew what he was doing. He longed for the doctor he knew at home. But he was helpless. There was nothing he could do. He thought about his mother who, of course, did not even know what had happened, and he prayed that his father would be all right before she would have to be told. He wondered with a dread bordering on horror what it would be like at home when his mother and the children received the news should his father not recover from his wounds. (He could not bring himself to form, even silently in his mind, the word *die*.) And he felt somehow guilty for even allowing such a thought to come into his head. He tried to pray, but he could not. And he kept seeing again vividly in his mind the crow dropping down to light on his father's shoulder, hearing again his mother's only slightly muted scream, her pleas, and her staunch insistence that the black bird had been a bad sign.

Jackson Gourd did not approve of the federal government's bullying infringement on the jurisdiction of the Cherokee Nation. He firmly believed that the Cherokee Nation had a good set of laws and the means of enforcing them, if only the United States would leave them alone and let them enforce the law. And he knew that under the laws of the United States, he had no jurisdiction over a crime that involved anyone who was not a Cherokee citizen. The cold, reasoning part of Gourd told him, therefore, to let the deputies do their own work. It was a nice irony when they needed his help, that their own law forbade his involvement; normally he enjoyed that irony. But there had been a brutal and cowardly shooting just on the edge of Tahlequah, and that came as a personal affront to Gourd, whose duty it was to maintain peace and tranquility in the small national capital. And in spite of his feelings about the federal government, he liked Dan Maples. Most people did. Gourd tried to think of someone who might have a reason to kill Maples.

Maples had come to the Cherokee Nation with a warrant for the arrest of *Wili Woyi*, or Bill Pigeon, for murder, but *Wili Woyi* was not a murderer. Gourd knew that. *Wili Woyi* had killed a prowler, a thief, at his own home. Nothing more would have come of it, except that it had been discovered later that the prowler had not been a Cherokee citizen. Therefore, the arrogant Judge Isaac C. Parker had issued a warrant for the arrest of *Wili Woyi* so that he could try him for murder in his own federal district court in Fort Smith. Gourd wondered briefly whether someone might have shot Maples in an effort to defend *Wili Woyi*, but he soon dismissed that thought as being highly improbable. Most Cherokees, like himself, figured that *Wili Woyi* could easily take care of himself. They considered it to be a good joke that anyone would actually try to capture the famous Indian doctor. He could make himself invisible. He could turn himself into an owl. How could they capture him? They would not even see him. No. It had to be something else, some other reason.

It was well known that Judge Parker's deputies carried blank warrants with them wherever they went. These warrants, commonly called whiskey warrants, were for use when the lawmen encountered any traffic in liquor, which was strictly forbidden in the entire area defined by the United States as Indian Territory. The Cherokee Nation had its own laws against liquor, but the United States court at Fort Smith was doing its best to take over that entire area of law enforcement, too. Perhaps a whiskey dealer had shot Maples. Jennie Shell was the only dealer in Tahlequah that Gourd knew about, but he was fairly certain that she would have had nothing to do with any shooting. He was also certain that the large influx of people caused by the council meeting had brought with it a number of dealers in liquor. He simply had not as yet been able to identify them. It didn't seem like much to go on, but the only other possibility that came to his mind was even more general and, therefore, less likely to lead anywhere, and that was that any Cherokee who resented the presence of federal agents inside the Cherokee Nation could be a suspect. That line of questioning would have placed Gourd himself on the list. He decided to pay a visit to Jennie Shell.

Ned Christie walked out of the woods and started down the west side of the main street of Tahlequah. He noticed the camp on the far side of the creek, but he thought nothing of it. Lots of people pitched tents and camped around Tahlequah during council meetings, because the two local hotels, the National and the Capitol, quickly filled up.

That was the reason he had come to town early. It was not a long walk from the edge of the woods on down into town, so Ned was soon lost in the crowd that was already bustling in the street. He wondered again how much of the morning he had lost. He was probably already late for the meeting. He crossed the street, dodging horses and wagons, and went into the hotel and up to his room.

George Jefferson put a hand on Sam Maples's shoulder.

"Sam," he said, "there's nothing more we can do here. The Doc's doing all he can. Me and Mack are

going out to see if we can find out who done this.
You want to come along, or you want to stay here?"

Sam wanted to get out of the room. He wanted to
do something, anything to get himself away from the
misery of just standing there, watching and feeling
helpless and afraid and sick.

"I'd better stay here with Papa, Mr. Jefferson," he
said. "When he wakes up, he'll want to see me."

"Okay, boy," said Jefferson. He gave Sam an
awkward pat on the back, nodded to Peel, and left
the room with Peel close behind.

Jackson Gourd called out to Jennie Shell in Cherokee, and she opened the door to peek out.

"Oh, it's you," she said, speaking English. "What
do you want? Those federal laws came to bother me
while ago. Now you come along. I ain't doing nothing but minding my own business."

"I came to talk about those federal lawmen, Jennie," said Gourd, switching to English. He knew that
Jennie could speak both languages. She was putting
him down, he figured, by speaking English to him,
placing him in the same category as the deputy marshals. Well, he'd go along.

"One of them was just shot out here," he said.
"Did you know that?"

"I heard shots," said Jennie. "I didn't look out.
It's safer to stay inside when folks're shooting at
each other."

"Well," said Gourd, "somebody shot Deputy Marshal Maples right down there at the footbridge. Do
you know Dan Maples?"

"He come by here," she said. "He was looking for Billy Pigeon. I don't know nothing 'bout Billy Pigeon."

"Was anybody else here when he stopped by?"

"There was another law with him. I don't know him."

"Was there anyone here with you?"

"No. I live by myself. Who'd be here?"

"Jennie," said Gourd, "I'm not trying to catch you. I don't want to arrest you. I'm not looking for whiskey, and I'm not interested in your business. Understand?"

"What business?" said Jennie. "I don't know what you're talking about."

"All right. All right. I'm just saying I'm not interested. Okay?"

Jennie looked at Gourd suspiciously for a moment.

"Okay," she said.

"I am interested in who might have shot Dan Maples, and it happened down here near your house. I want to know who's been around."

"Them two laws come by this morning," said Jennie. "No one else."

"Who else is in town selling whiskey?"

"What do you mean who else? I ain't selling no whiskey. What do you mean?"

"Jennie," said Gourd, his voice more firm than before, "I told you I'm not after you. A federal lawman's been shot. It might have been a whiskey peddler who did it. Do you know of anyone in town?"

"There's a white man out south," she said. "Out

on the road to Fort Gibson. That's what I heard.
Everyone's going out there. He's got lower prices
than . . . Well, that's where they're going to buy
whiskey. I only seen two men up here all yesterday
evening."

"Who were they?" said Gourd.

"John Parris and Ned Christie."

"Ned Christie, the councilor?" said Gourd.

"That was him. I seen him before. And John Parris."

"Did they buy—uh, did they have any whiskey?"

"I think they did," said Jennie. "I think maybe I
seen a bottle they had."

Jefferson and Peel poked around the big tree the
gunman had hidden behind, but they found no evidence there. They walked into the woods, moving
cautiously. The man might still be in there somewhere. As they moved farther into the trees, they
separated slightly. Peel, nervous, drew his revolver.
He took slow, careful steps, trying not to make any
noise, but he was not successful at that. He looked
at the ground, and he looked up and around. He did
not know just what he was looking for. He stepped
into a small clearing and saw an empty bottle on the
ground. He looked around. No one was anywhere to
be seen. He heard off to his left the sound of footsteps, and he called out in a low voice, "George?"

"What is it, Mack?" answered Jefferson. "You
find something?"

"Over here."

Jefferson made his way to the clearing where Peel

was waiting, and Peel pointed to the bottle. Jefferson picked it up and sniffed it. The whiskey smell was still strong.

"I'd say someone laid out here last night," he said.

Gourd crossed the creek and found Cookie at the deputies' camp alone. He had some coffee made, so Gourd took a cup and sat down.

"Where's all the others?" Gourd asked.

"Sam's staying with Mr. Maples," said Cookie. "Mr. Jefferson and Mr. Peel went into the woods over there to look around."

Gourd nodded and took a sip of the hot coffee. It was good. He liked it like that, out by a campfire. The camp was well made and well situated, a comfortable camp. It would have been pleasant, had it not been for the fact that he could turn his head only slightly and see the spot where Maples had fallen into the creek with three bullets in his back. He finished the coffee and set the cup down just as Jefferson and Peel emerged from the woods, and he got up and walked to meet them on the other side of the creek.

"What you got there?" he said.

Jefferson held up the bottle for Gourd to see.

"Found it out there," he said. "Someone drank it in there just a little ways. Last night, I'd guess."

"Jennie Shell sold a bottle to John Parris and Ned Christie yesterday afternoon," said Gourd. "I bet that's the one. Ned wouldn't want to take any chances on being seen with it. I mean, more than most. He's on the council, you know. He'd go right into the closest hiding place, I imagine."

"Ned Christie," said Jefferson. "I've heard of him. He's some kind of a troublemaker, ain't he?"

"I suppose that depends on your point of view," said Gourd. "He speaks up for the rights of Cherokees, and he supports the sovereignty of the Cherokee Nation."

"Does that mean he's against the United States?" asked Peel.

"On some issues," said Gourd, "I guess it does."

"Well," said Jefferson, "Judge Parker don't have a very high opinion of him. I know that much."

Gourd thought it best to refrain from voicing his own opinion of Judge Parker.

"Well," he said, "I suppose we ought to find both Ned and John. They were probably down here. They might have seen something or heard something that could help us figure this thing out."

"If they were drunk," said Peel, "they might have done the shooting."

"I doubt it, Mr. Peel," said Gourd. "Ned Christie is one of our most respected citizens."

"And he was sneaking around in the woods drinking whiskey," said Peel.

"A lawmaker and breaking the law," said Jefferson. "Where will we find them?"

"Ned should be at the council meeting. There's no telling where John is just now, but we can check his house. It's not far."

"Let's go then," said Jefferson.

"Where to?"

"To the council meeting."

Chapter 4

They went to the capitol and found out that Ned Christie was absent from the meeting. That information only served to strengthen the suspicion of the deputies regarding Ned's guilt.

"He could be missing for any number of reasons," said Gourd, and he thought, *We know that he helped finish off a bottle of whiskey yesterday. He could still be sleeping it off*, but he didn't want to say that to the two white men.

Jefferson grunted. The three lawmen walked across the yard of the capitol building and headed back toward the street. Gourd touched Jefferson's arm lightly.

"Don't get excited," he said. "Just keep walking."

"What?" said Jefferson. "What is it?"

"John Parris."

"Where?"

"If we just keep walking," said Gourd, "we'll meet him right across the street."

"Which one is he?" said Peel.

Gourd didn't tell them. He was afraid they'd draw their guns and rush at Parris, causing Parris to run or, if he was armed, to start shooting. These federal lawmen had a way of creating panic around them. He kept quiet and kept walking. They made their way through the heavy traffic to the other side of the street, and Gourd stepped in the way of a man who was walking south.

"Hello, John," he said.

John Parris stopped and looked at the policeman. He appeared to be slightly nervous.

"Hello, Jackson," he said, with a forced smile. "How are you?"

"Doing fine, John," said Gourd. "Just fine. I want you to meet some friends of mine."

"Oh," said Parris. "Sure."

"This is George Jefferson, and this here is Mack Peel. George and Mack are U.S. deputy marshals. They rode in here with Dan Maples this morning. You know Dan Maples?"

"I've heard of him," said Parris.

"Gentlemen," said Gourd, "this is John Parris. John, we'd like to talk to you. Ask you a few questions."

Parris became more nervous. He looked over his shoulder and then back at the lawmen.

"What about?" he said.

"Let's go someplace where we can talk," said Gourd.

"Let's go up to our camp," said Jefferson.

"That all right with you, John?" said Gourd.

"Well," said Parris, "I got some things to do. I—yeah. Sure. It's all right."

They had Parris sit on a log on one side of the campfire, and the three lawmen sat facing him across the fire. Cookie milled around, feeling a little superfluous.

"Have a cup of coffee, John?" said Gourd.

"No," said Parris. "No, thanks. I . . . Well, all right."

Cookie poured a cup of coffee and handed it to Parris, who set it on the ground between his feet. Gourd also got a cup, but the two deputies did not. They were intense.

"John," said Gourd, "we know you bought a bottle of whiskey from Jennie Shell yesterday."

Parris opened his mouth as if to say something, but Gourd stopped him with a gesture.

"Just hold on," he said. "Wait till I'm done. All right? We know that much. And we know that Ned Christie was with you. Did you go into the woods right over there?"

"I—uh—I don't know," said Parris.

"What the hell do you mean, you don't know?" said Jefferson. "Did you go in there or didn't you?"

"Yeah," said Parris, flinching. "Yeah. For a little bit."

"With Ned?" said Gourd.

"Yeah."

"How long were you in there, John?" said Gourd.

"I don't know."

Parris had begun to sweat. He rubbed his hands

together and kept looking around, as if he were looking for someone to come to his aid. He picked up the coffee cup from between his feet.

"All night?"

"It was late when I left. I don't know what time. I can't remember."

"Did Ned leave with you?"

"Yes. No."

"Which one?" said Jefferson.

"No. He didn't," said Parris.

"John," said Gourd, "did you see anyone else around here? Did you see or hear anything unusual?"

"I didn't see nothing, Jackson," said Parris.

Jefferson stood up and walked around the fire to stand behind Parris. Parris's agitation became intense.

"What's this all about?" he said. "You going to arrest me for drinking?"

"We don't give a damn about your drinking," said Jefferson from behind Parris. "Do you own a gun?"

"No. Well, yeah. I got a gun at home."

"What kind of gun?"

"Shotgun."

"You don't own a handgun?"

"No."

"Was Ned Christie armed last night?"

"I don't know."

"John," said Gourd, "where were you early this morning?"

"I was around. I don't know. Around town."

"Did you know that Dan Maples was shot this morning? Right over there. He was walking across the footbridge, and someone shot him in the back three times from over there in the woods. Did you know about that, John?"

"I heard about it in town."

"Did you do it?" said Jefferson.

"No."

"Did Ned Christie do it?"

"I don't know. I didn't know nothing about it. I heard about it in town. Just a little while ago. That's all."

"You mean to say that you were in town," said Peek, "and you didn't hear the shots? There were five shots fired. You didn't hear them?"

"No. I mean, I might have heard them, but I didn't know anybody got shot. Not till later."

"You and Ned Christie were the only people we know of in those woods," said Jefferson. "If you didn't shoot Dan, then Christie did. Is that right?"

"I didn't do it."

"Then Christie had to do it. Right?"

"I don't know. I guess so. Yeah. Ned done it. I guess Ned done it. I didn't see it."

"You hear that, Mack?" said Jefferson.

"He said Ned Christie done it," said Peel.

"Wait a minute," said Gourd.

Jefferson grabbed Parris by the shirt collar and pulled him to his feet.

"Get on out of here," he said. "Go on."

Parris looked unsure for an instant. Then he ran.

"What did you let him go for?" said Gourd.

"We're interested in something a lot bigger than

a whiskey violation here, Gourd," said Jefferson. "We got what we wanted out of him."

"You're not taking what he just said as gospel, are you?" said Gourd.

"It's not just that," said Jefferson. "Look. Ned Christie hates the United States. He got drunk yesterday right over there in the woods. Someone shot Dan this morning from right over there. Ned Christie's absent from the council meeting this morning, and John Parris says that Ned Christie shot Dan. What the hell more do you want?"

"I'd like something more substantial than what you just got out of Parris," said Gourd.

"Well, it's out of your hands, Gourd," said Jefferson. "It ain't your worry. Thanks for your help."

Ned Christie had cleaned himself up and put on fresh clothes. Leaving his guns in the hotel room, he headed for the capitol building. He had reached the grounds when he saw Jackson Gourd come hurrying out of the building. Gourd rushed over to Ned and spoke to him in Cherokee.

"Nede," he said, "you have to get out of town."

"Why?" asked Ned. "I have this meeting to go to."

"Dan Maples was shot this morning down at the creek. He's hurt bad. Two deputy marshals intend to arrest you for the shooting."

"Why?" said Ned. "What makes them think I did it?"

Gourd hesitated for a moment, but he knew that he had to get Ned out of town in a hurry.

"John Parris said so," he said. "Now just get out of town. They won't listen to reason."

"Okay," said Ned. "Thanks, friend."

He turned toward the street, but Gourd grabbed him by the arm.

"Not that way, Ned. Go behind the building. You know my horse? The big brown one?"

"Yes."

"He's back there saddled. Take him. They might be watching the stable. Go on, now."

Ned slapped Gourd on the back and ran around behind the capitol. He found Gourd's horse saddled and waiting, mounted it and rode to the rear of the National Hotel. He hurried inside through the back door and got his guns and blanket roll from the room. Then he went back outside, mounted up again, and rode east out of Tahlequah toward the hills, toward home.

Jackson Gourd was a man sworn to uphold the law, and he had just helped a fugitive avoid arrest. He did not feel guilty, however, because he thought that the federal officers had taken a tremendous leap in logic to reach their conclusions. The evidence against Ned Christie was circumstantial at best, even scanty, and Gourd did not believe that Ned was guilty. He knew Ned Christie and respected him. It was true that Ned Christie hated the United States for what it was doing to the Cherokee Nation, but Ned was fighting the United States as a politician. He would not shoot a man in the back. And for no purpose. What possible good could the death of Dan

Maples do the Cherokee Nation? Gourd would not, could not believe that Ned had done it. And Gourd did not feel guilty because, even though he was sworn to uphold the law, it was Cherokee law to which he was sworn. He felt no obligation to uphold United States law. On that issue he agreed with Ned Christie totally. Well, he had warned Ned, and now it was really, as George Jefferson had said, out of his hands. But Gourd had a dark feeling. The shooting of Maples was bad, but things were going to get worse—much worse—before it was all over.

Ned watched over his shoulder the first few miles out of Tahlequah, and he ran Jackson Gourd's horse pretty hard, but when he felt reasonably sure that no one was following him, he relaxed a little and eased up on the horse. He was perplexed. Someone had shot Maples, and the deputy marshals wanted to arrest him for the crime. Why? John Parris had accused him. Why, he wondered, would John have done that? They had gotten drunk together. They were friends. It didn't make any sense. Had John killed the lawman and then blamed Ned to cover for himself? No. Ned could not imagine that of John. John was not a killer, not even a fighter. And John didn't even carry a gun. Ned could not figure out any reason for John Parris to have named him as the gunman who shot Maples. It was probably all a mistake of some kind, and he would find a way to straighten it out.

Ned didn't know Dan Maples. He had heard of him, but he wasn't even sure that he could put the right face with the name. He had not heard anything bad about the man, except for the fact that he was one of the army of deputy marshals that Judge Parker sent out to patrol the "Indian Territory." If Maples was a good man, then it was too bad he had been shot, but because of his profession, Ned couldn't feel too much remorse for the man. He had no business in the Cherokee Nation anyway, wearing his badge, carrying his guns, enforcing the laws of a foreign country.

But to be wrongly accused of having shot the man in the back, that was bad. And by a friend. John Parris. Ned would have to get to the bottom of that. He couldn't just go back into Tahlequah and start to investigate this problem. The deputies would be there. He'd have to send someone else, a friend or relative maybe. Someone he could trust.

He wondered what was happening at the council meeting, and he wished that he could be there. If he hadn't gone with John Parris to drink whiskey, he thought, none of this would have happened. He knew better than to drink whiskey. Whiskey was bad. It was one of the many bad things the white man had brought to the Indians. Ned had a moment of anger against himself for the foolishness of getting drunk, but he let it pass. Regrets over things that were over and done were useless. He would simply try not to make more mistakes in the future.

John Parris, he thought. *Why did John Parris say that wrong thing about me?*

"Come on, Sam," said Mack Peel. "You've got to eat something, boy. You ain't doing no good here anyway."

Blake looked up from where he sat at Dan Maples's bedside.

"Go on, son," he said. "I'll let you know if there's any change."

Sam stood up from the straight-backed chair against the wall. He looked bewildered.

"Where will we go, Mack?" he asked.

"Up to the camp. Cookie's getting a meal ready for us. Come on."

"You know where our camp is, Doc?" said Sam. "That's where I'll be if you need me."

"I know," said Blake.

"I won't be gone long."

"All right."

"Come on, Sam," said Peel.

They went outside and walked up to the camp. Sam moved as if he were in a daze. He hesitated at the footbridge, and Peel had to encourage him to cross. Jefferson and Cookie were already at the camp, and they got Sam seated. Cookie gave him a plate of eggs, bacon, and potatoes, and he poured him a cup of coffee. Sam had not thought he'd be able to eat, but he surprised himself and ate like a hog. When he finished, he got himself another cup of coffee.

"How's your daddy doing?" asked Cookie.

There was a moment of hushed silence.

"No change," said Sam. "Did anyone pick up his gun?"

"I did," said Peel. "It's around here somewhere."

"Right here," said Cookie. He ducked inside a tent and came out with the revolver, holding it out for Sam. "I dried it off and oiled it," he added.

"Thanks, Cookie," said Sam. "Just keep it in there for now, will you?"

"Sure."

"Mr. Jefferson?" said Sam.

"Yeah?" said Jefferson.

"Do you know who did it?"

"Yeah," said Jefferson. "It was an Indian named Ned Christie."

"Have you caught him?"

"Not yet."

Sam stared into the campfire for a long, silent moment. He took a sip of his coffee, then put the cup down.

"Ned Christie," he said. "Well, thanks for the food, Cookie. That was real good. Right now I'd better get back to Papa."

Chapter 5

Ned's family reacted to the news from Tahlequah exactly as he had imagined they would: Arch with anger and defiance; Gatey with worry disguised as reserved resignation to fate. The Cherokees had come to expect this sort of thing from the United States government. They had signed their first treaty with the invading, English-speaking white men in 1721. That treaty, between the Cherokees and South Carolina, had been an exchange of Cherokee land for a promise of perpetual peace, friendship, and protection. It was nullified, of course, by the American Revolution.

In 1785, the Cherokees signed a treaty with the United States: the Treaty of Hopewell. Again there was the promise of perpetual peace and friendship. The boundaries between the two nations were described, and the United States promised to remove its protection from any U.S. citizen who attempted to settle on Cherokee land. The "Indians," it said, "may punish him or not as they please." That treaty and all its promises lasted only six years. In 1791 the United States insisted on negotiating a new treaty with the Cherokees. In the Treaty of Holston, all of the Cherokee land in Kentucky was taken by the United States as well as additional land elsewhere. The old promise of perpetual friendship and peace was renewed, as well as the promise to keep white settlers off of remaining Cherokee land. The treaty "solemnly guaranteed" remaining Cherokee land.

Still more treaties followed hard and fast: the Treaty of Tellico Garrison, 1804; a second Treaty of Tellico Garrison, 1805; the Treaty of Washington, 1806; the Treaty of Chickasaw Old Fields, 1807; the Treaty of Cherokee Agency, 1817; a second Treaty of Washington, 1819; a third Treaty of Washington, 1828. Each of these treaties repeated the same promises, promises that had never been kept by the United States, and with each treaty the United States took more Cherokee land. This incredible succession of treaties reduced the size of the Cherokee Nation to half of what it had been before the American Revolution. In exchange for the lost land, more than four million acres, the Cherokee Nation received from the United States $240,700.

Then came the Treaty of New Echota. Designed to take away all remaining Cherokee land in the East in exchange for land out west in what would soon become known as "Indian Territory," the Treaty of New Echota was signed in 1835, not by any official representatives of the Cherokee Nation, but by a group of private Cherokee citizens willing to cooperate with the United States. The Trail of Tears followed. Cherokees were seized in their own homes, dragged out, and herded into stockade prisons where they were held until the time to be marched out west. Thousands died along the way. But the treaty "guaranteed" the new western land, once the Cherokees had been removed. It further promised, as had all the others before, perpetual peace and friendship, and it assured the Cherokees that they would never again be disturbed in their new country.

The Treaty of New Echota also promised that the United States would "protect the Cherokee nation from domestic strife and foreign enemies and against intestine wars between the several tribes." Yet when the southern states seceded from the Union to form the Confederate States of America, thus precipitating the Civil War, the United States did not "protect the Cherokee nation." A faction of Cherokees joined with the new C.S.A. and proceeded to ravage the Cherokee Nation. Principal Chief John Ross wrote letters to the United States begging them to send troops to protect the neutrality of the Cherokee Nation, as they were obligated by treaty to do. The United States refused to comply, and Chief Ross was forced to sign a treaty with the Confederate States, a treaty that the United States later used as a convenient excuse to nullify all previous treaties.

A new treaty was forced on the Cherokees in 1866. It compelled the Cherokee Nation to give equal rights of citizenship to all former slaves "as well as all free colored persons who were in the country at the commencement of the rebellion." It forced the Cherokee Nation to grant a railroad right of way. It called for a census of all Cherokees. It took away land from the Cherokee Nation. It gave to United States courts jurisdiction over all cases, civil or criminal, involving anyone not a Cherokee citizen, and it guaranteed "to the people of the Cherokee Nation the quiet and peaceable possession of their country and protection against domestic feuds and insurrections, and against hostilities of other tribes."

A short twenty-one years had passed, and already there were more whites than Indians in the Cherokee Nation. Many of them were illegal squatters, many were in railroad towns along the twenty-mile-wide right of way the Cherokee Nation had been forced to grant, and others had married Cherokees. The United States Congress had passed the Dawes Act, or General Allotment Act, calling for the breaking up of tribally owned land and the assigning of small farms to individual tribal members. There was a loud, nationwide cry for statehood for "Indian Territory" and "Oklahoma Territory," and the Cherokee Nation's government was dominated by mixed-bloods whose world-view was like that of the white man.

The Cherokees had come to expect this sort of thing at the hands of the United States. Ned got out all his guns and checked them and cleaned them. He made sure they were all loaded and that extra ammunition was handy. The guns were placed in convenient locations around the house: behind the door, near windows. He would be prepared for an attack by the deputies. But he was not guilty. He knew he was not guilty, and he had some sense of the operation of the law. He sat down and composed a letter to Judge Isaac C. Parker at Fort Smith. He proclaimed to the judge his innocence and requested time to prove it, and he gave it to a friend to post. (The letter was never answered.) Then he went on about his business at home.

Young Sam looked forward to one of two very different moments. He looked forward to the moment when his father would open his eyes and see him waiting there in the room. "Hi, Sam," he would say, and Sam would rush to his bedside, tears of joy in his eyes, and Dan would say, "It's going to be all right, son." And it would be. It would be all right because Dan had said so. Sam could almost hear him saying that. He had heard it so many times before, and every time, he had believed it, and always Dan had been right. All that was required in Sam's world to make everything all right was for Dan to say that it would be so. Sam waited anxiously for Dan to come around and say it once more, this most important time of all.

But his imagination forced another possible future moment into his consciousness, and this one Sam anticipated with horror. For the other possibility was that Dan would not wake up, would never again open his eyes, would never speak again. Sam hated to imagine that moment, the moment when death would come into the strange and lonely room in which he waited, watching over his bloody and un-

conscious father. He hated himself for even considering that as a possibility. He tried to concentrate on
that other moment, the one in which Dan would
open his eyes and smile and speak and say that
everything would be all right, but he could not pre-
vent the thoughts of doom, the images of horror.

Then the dream would expand, and Sam would
see himself as a dark and brooding avenger, stalking
the evil Ned Christie to the far reaches of the world.
He would find himself on a barren, colorless waste-
land, and he would be dressed in black, and he
would have two guns strapped around his waist. He
would be sporting a black mustache, and he would
be a man. And up ahead through a mist, he would
see a large, dark figure looming. It would come
closer, moving slowly and deliberately, and it would
be Ned Christie. And the figure of Ned Christie
would be vague, but it would be evil.

The snarling, evil figure would make a sudden
move, reaching for its weapons, but Sam would be
faster. His guns would appear in his hands as if by
magic, and he would fire them both, alternately, until
they were empty, and every shot he fired would rip
through the writhing, twisting figure of evil until it
was a bloody mess, and with a final agonized bellow,
it would pitch forward to lie lifeless on the sterile
waste. And Sam would feel a surge of manly pride
in his imaginary role, and then he would feel guilty
for taking a kind of pleasure in his father's death,
and he would try to force the image of the happy
moment back into his primary thoughts.

When the moment came, it was not dramatic at

all. Dan Maples just stopped breathing. That was all. Sam had been up, sitting in the room most of the time, for most of a day and all of a night. It was early morning, almost twenty-four hours after the shooting, and Dan Maples just stopped breathing. Dr. Blake had been sitting at the bedside. Sam was in the chair against the wall. Blake looked over his shoulder at Sam, sitting there stiffly, looking very young and very scared.

"I'm sorry, son," he said. "He's gone."

Sam did not move, did not respond. The wild images, both the exultant and the violent, were gone from his mind. They were replaced by a dull and listless stupor. He sat and he stared. Blake stood up and pulled the sheet up over Dan Maples's head. He looked at Sam for a moment, then he left the room. Sam sat and stared. In a few moments, Blake returned with George Jefferson. Jefferson walked over to the bed and lifted the sheet for a look. Then he replaced it and turned to Sam.

"Come on, Sam," he said. "There's nothing you can do here now."

"Where?" said Sam. "Come on where?"

"Back to the camp. We'll pack up. We got to take him home now."

"What about Ned Christie?" said Sam.

"We'll go to Marshal Carroll when we get back to Fort Smith and tell him what happened here. He'll get a warrant from Judge Parker for the arrest of Ned Christie, and then a posse will come after him. They'll get him, Sam. You can be sure of that."

"I want to be in that posse," said Sam.

"Well," said Jefferson, "I know how you feel, boy, but I don't think they'll let you. They'll say you're too young."

"He killed my father," said Sam, and then he lost his voice in sudden, convulsive sobs.

Jackson Gourd still thought that the deputies were probably wrong, certainly hasty, in laying the blame for Maples's death on Ned Christie. In Gourd's mind, Ned Christie was not just a politician, he was a statesman. He was a Cherokee patriot. He was an honorable man who made an honest living, but he also gave his time and energy and his considerable talents for the good of his people. Gourd had heard Ned Christie make speeches. He had heard him explain to people the rights of the Cherokee Nation as a sovereign state. He had listened while Ned Christie related the origins of the Cherokee people, and then catalogued the slow, deliberate invasion of the white race from Europe. He recited for the people the long, seemingly endless series of treaties forced on the Cherokees by the United States, and he told them of all the broken promises made in those treaties. But most important of all, he told them of the treaties that were current and the promises contained in them. And he told them what rights they had as a sovereign nation under those treaties. They did not have to allow the United States government to divide up their land the way it was doing to other tribes. And they did not have to submit to being swallowed up and dismantled by statehood.

No, Jackson Gourd did not believe that Ned

Christie was a skulking murderer, and for that reason, he was on his way to Ned Christie's house. Ned Christie had to know that Maples was dead. The pursuit would be more intense. Judge Parker would want him desperately, and the deputies would be almost fanatical in hunting down a man they believed had killed one of their own. But they had been so willing, so anxious to believe. Gourd still could not get over how easily they had decided that Ned was guilty. Did they really not care? Did they need a scapegoat so badly? Was Ned Christie such a powerful enemy of the United States that even a cold-blooded murderer of a deputy United States marshal paled beside him? Was it more important to get Ned Christie than to bring the real killer to justice? Gourd could not figure the deputies' motives, but all of this, he would tell Ned. He could do that much.

He was a little uneasy riding up to Ned Christie's house. He was a lawman, and Ned was wanted by the law. Was it possible that Ned would misinterpret his visit? He didn't really think so, although the thought was in his mind. However, as he approached the house, he saw Ned standing in front, waiting.

" *'Siyo*, Jackson," said Ned.

" *'Siyo, Nede,"* said Gourd. Noting that the conversation would take place in Cherokee, Gourd dismounted and let the reins trail on the ground. "I'm sorry about what happened in town," he said.

"It wasn't your doing," said Ned, "and you warned me to get away. I'm in your debt. Do you want some coffee?"

"Yes," said Gourd. "Thanks."

"Gatey," Ned called over his shoulder. "Jackson Gourd is here. We'd like some coffee."

"I'll bring some," Gatey answered from inside the house.

"Sit down," said Ned.

Two wooden, cane-bottomed chairs stood against the front wall of the house. Gourd walked over to one and sat down. Ned took the other. Soon Gatey came out with the coffee.

"Thank you," said Gourd. "How are you?"

"I'm well," said Gatey. "Thanks. And you?"

"Pretty good. How's your son doing?"

"Growing big," said Gatey, She excused herself and left the two men alone to talk.

"Ned," said Gourd, "I came out to tell you that Maples died this morning."

"Ah, that's too bad," said Ned.

"Yes. Now the charge will be murder. The murder of a federal lawman."

"I've written a letter to Judge Parker," said Ned. "I told him that I'm innocent, and I asked him to give me some time to prove it."

Gourd sipped some hot coffee.

"I don't think he'll answer your letter," he said, "but if he does, he'll tell you to give yourself up and prove your innocence in court."

"In federal court?" said Ned. "His court?"

"Yes."

"What do you think, my friend?"

"Since I'm a lawman," said Gourd, "I should tell you to do that. Give yourself up and go to court. That would be the proper advice for me to give."

Ned waited. Gourd was silent for a long moment, staring into his cup of steaming coffee, a concerned wrinkle on his brow.

"But since I'm a Cherokee," he finally continued, "my advice is to stay away from that federal court. Those deputies have already decided that you're the killer. I'd say at least wait for Parker's reaction. Let's see if he issues a warrant for your arrest on the word of those deputies and their flimsy evidence."

"That's what I was going to do anyway," said Ned with a smile, "but I'm glad that your advice agrees with my intentions."

Again there was silence. The two men sat sipping their coffee. Then Gourd finished his and put down the cup. He stood up and walked to his horse. Picking up the reins, he turned back toward Ned.

"Be careful," he said. "I believe there will be a warrant for you. I believe that it's because of your politics. It's a way to shut you up. John Parris didn't accuse you. He's weak, and they frightened him and put words in his mouth. So they say that he accused you and that he's an eyewitness."

"I'm glad you told me that," said Ned. "I wondered why John had said that about me."

Gourd swung up into his saddle.

"I'll try to keep you informed," he said.

"No," said Ned. "You've done enough. It won't be good for you if it becomes known that you're riding out here to see me. I have friends who will go into town now and then to hear the news. From now on, you keep to yourself and play the lawman's role."

"Good luck, Ned," said Gourd. He turned his horse and headed back toward Tahlequah. Ned stood and watched him go. There was a real friend. It made Ned feel good to know that a lawman would come to warn him, to help him in this matter. But of course, Ned himself was a lawmaker. These people who were after him were invaders and conquerors, the common enemy. He knew that Jackson Gourd felt the same way he did on that issue. Well, he did not know how this business would turn out, but he did know one thing. He would never surrender to the federal lawmen.

Chapter 6

Isaac Parker stood at the window in his office, up-stairs in the old stone building that had been the Fort Smith commissary. He stood with his hands clasped behind his back and stared out at the combination jail and courthouse that stood one hundred or so yards to the southwest. Things would be much better when the new courthouse was done. Then he would have his office in the same building as the courtroom and both of them a safe distance away from the noise and stench of the prison. The new building would be closer to his home as well, and his walk to work and back each day would therefore be shortened. That, of course, was not the judge's main concern, but it was a thought that gave him a certain amount of pleasure to contemplate. He had put on a few pounds in the ten years since he had arrived to preside over the federal court for the Western District of Arkansas. The first few years the walk had not been bad. He had actually enjoyed it, except on those days when the mud had been ankle deep. That was no longer a problem, for Parker had prevailed upon the city to provide sidewalks, but his walks had become tiresome, wearying, and, he had noticed lately, a bit painful. About halfway between his house and his office, his breathing would become labored, and he would feel pain in the joints of his hips.

Yes, he thought, the ten years had aged him. His once dark hair and beard now showed streaks of gray. He took a deep breath and felt his belly stretch the cloth of his vest on either side of the buttons. It was a tough and demanding job, but it was also a job he had actively sought. And it was a job with a mission. The five nations of Indians that made up the Indian Territory were struggling to create small, civilized states, but it had become obvious that they were woefully incapable of making the great transition from dark savagery to enlightened civilization alone. Lawlessness was rampant in the nations. For that reason the United States government had established the court at Fort Smith and had given it jurisdiction over the Indian Territory. And Parker had practically begged for the appointment. He had achieved it, and he had taken to it with nearly religious zeal.

And now he watched through the window. He had a particularly troubling case at hand. One of his deputies had just been killed over in the Cherokee Nation, it seemed by a full-blood Cherokee agitator named Ned Christie. Parker had heard of Christie, an elected Cherokee official who was known for making inflammatory speeches calculated to stir up the backward full bloods. And the murdered deputy had been Dan Maples, a good man, one of the best. This problem had to be dealt with quickly and surely. Parker knew that George Jefferson and Mack Peel, deputies, were over there in Carroll's office just above the old jail and between the courtroom and the new row of cells. They would be telling the marshal about the shooting. As soon as they were done, Carroll was to report to the judge's office and fill him in on the details. Parker watched for the deputies to leave the building.

He turned and paced away from the window, going all the way across the room to the door. For a brief moment, he considered going down the stairs and across the yard to Carroll's office, but his hips were hurting him already, so he dismissed the thought. He turned and walked over to his desk and picked up a letter that was lying there. He gave it a quick glance and dropped it back down on the desk top. Then he returned to the window. He saw Jefferson and Peel leaving the building across the way, and less than a minute later, Carroll emerged and headed toward the old commissary. Parker got behind his desk and sat down to await the arrival of the marshal.

It didn't take long. Carroll appeared in the doorway and stretched his neck looking in at Parker. The judge was shuffling papers, looking busy. He picked up the letter once more, then raised his eyebrows and looked over it at Carroll standing in the doorway.

"Come in, Mr. Carroll," he said.

The marshal walked in, his hat in his hands, and stood in front of the desk.

"Sit down," said Parker.

Carroll sat.

"Mr. Carroll," said Parker, "I have here a very interesting letter. It arrived only this morning. It's from a Mr. Ned Christie in the Cherokee Nation and was apparently posted in Tahlequah. It's a rather bold letter, written in a firm, quite legible hand. Mr. Christie is obviously well educated."

"Yes, sir," said Carroll.

"That, of course, makes what he did all the more inexcusable."

"Uh, yes, sir," said Carroll.

"Dan Maples was a fine officer," said the judge. "A fine officer. And a good man."

"He was a good friend, Your Honor."

"His loss is tragic. He leaves behind a wife and six children, not to mention a vacancy in our ranks that will be hard to fill."

Carroll fidgeted nervously with his hat.

"Young Sam wants to try to fill it," he said, "according to what George said. George Jefferson."

"Sam?"

"Dan's oldest boy. Sam Maples."

"How old is the boy?" asked the judge.

"He's sixteen, sir. Too young yet."

"Yes. He'll have to wait a few years. In the meantime, keep an eye on him, Mr. Carroll."

"Yes, sir."

Parker stood up and paced to his window. He

stared out at the combination prison and courtroom and the six-man gallows just beyond.

"Did he do it, Mr. Carroll?" he said.

"Sir?"

Parker turned back around to face Carroll. "Is there any doubt," he said, "concerning the guilt of Ned Christie?"

"Oh. Well, sir, George Jefferson and Dan were crossing a footbridge just outside of Tahlequah when it happened. Their camp was just a little ways on down the creek there. Somebody stepped out from behind a tree and shot poor Dan in the back, then run. None of them saw the man. Not even George. He was the closest. Well, they determined that a woman named Shell whose house is right near there had sold some whiskey the night before to John Parris and Ned Christie. They found the bottle in the woods near where the shooting took place, and they found Parris and questioned him. He said Ned Christie did the shooting. Christie had already took off."

Parker stepped back over to the chair behind his desk and sat down. He pulled open a drawer and took out a printed form. He placed the form carefully on the desk in front of him, picked up his pen and dipped it in the inkwell. On one blank space he wrote, "Ned Christie, a Cherokee Indian," on another, "for the murder of Daniel Maples, a deputy U.S. marshal, on May 4, 1887, in Tahlequah, I.T.," and on still another, he signed his own name. He pressed a blotter to the ink and handed the paper to Carroll.

"Get this taken care of right away," he said.

"Yes, sir."

"Who will you send?"

"Heck Thomas and Larry Isbel are available," said Carroll.

"They're good men," said Parker. "How soon will they leave?"

"First thing in the morning, sir."

"Good. Mr. Carroll."

"Yes, sir?"

"Deputy Maples was the sixty-fourth deputy killed in the line of duty in the Indian Territory. Ned Christie has got to be brought to justice."

"Thomas and Isbel are two of the best men we've got, sir. They'll bring him in."

"One way or the other, Mr. Carroll," said Parker.

"Sir?"

"Alive—or dead."

Heck Thomas was a native Georgian who had served as a courier in the Confederate Army during the Civil War when he was only twelve years old. Isaac Parker had found him working as a private detective in Texas in 1886 and brought him to Fort Smith as one of his deputies. In his mid-thirties, Thomas sported a shaggy walrus mustache. He strolled around Fort Smith in corduroy trousers stuffed into the high tops of fancy, stitched boots. His flannel shirt was buttoned all the way up to the top button, and a short, wide tie tied in a four-in-hand was tacked to the front of his shirt by a pearl stickpin. His pearl-handled six-shooter in its tooled leather holster was held by the same belt that held up his trousers and was worn just to the right of his fly. The star inside a half-moon that denoted his status as deputy United States marshal was pinned to the shirt front low and to the left. On his head was a round-crowned, flat-brimmed hat. Thomas usually carried with him in his right hand either his Winchester rifle or a sawed-off shotgun. He was obviously an image-conscious man, one who enjoyed playing the role of feared and dangerous, gun-fighting lawman.

L. P. Isbel was not so flamboyant. But when he met Thomas early in the morning prepared to travel to Tahlequah in the Cherokee Nation to search out Ned Christie, wanted for the murder of Dan Maples, he came well armed. Isbel was a plain and practical man with a cool head. Marshal Carroll had thought that the two would make a good combination, and apparently Parker had agreed. Carroll had sent for the two as soon as he had gotten back to his office following his meeting with the judge. When they had arrived, he had handed the warrant to Thomas. Thomas had unfolded the paper and read out loud.

"Ned Christie," he had said. "A Cherokee Indian. The man that killed Dan Maples."

"That's right," Carroll had answered. "I don't have to tell you how important this one is."

"Do we know where to find him?" Isbel had asked.

"I'd say start in Tahlequah," Carroll had said. "He's well known there. He's on the Cherokee council. I'd say start out by finding out where he lives and then go check out his house."

"You think a wanted killer would just set home and wait for us?" Thomas had asked.

"You never know, Heck," Carroll had answered. "These Cherokees are funny people. You might find him there. Even if you don't, you might find some family or neighbors, somebody you can question. It's a place to start."

"All right," Thomas had said, folding up the paper and tucking it inside his shirt. He and Isbel had been on their way out of Carroll's office when Carroll had spoken one last time.

"Heck," he had said, "you have the authority to take on up to three more men. Your choice. But get started first thing in the morning."

So Thomas and Isbel were going to Tahlequah to begin their investigation. Their plan was to ask questions until they determined the location of Ned Christie's home. Then they would go to his home. From there they would play it by ear. If they found him there, they would attempt to arrest him. If he resisted arrest, they would be prepared to fight. If, on the other hand, their prey was not at home, they would question anyone else they might find there in an effort to determine where he might have gone. It was a simple plan of action, and it was all the plan they had.

Sam Maples thought about going to see Marshal Carroll for permission to join the posse that was going after Ned Christie. He thought about delivering an impassioned speech to Carroll about now it was not only his right as Dan Maples's oldest son but also his duty. He even rehearsed the speech over and over in his mind.

"You care about it," he would say, "because he was a deputy and maybe because he was a friend of yours. And it's your job. But he was my father. Do you know what it's like to see your own father shot down? To watch him die? He couldn't even talk to me. Marshal Carroll, I have to go."

He held Dan Maples's six-gun in his hands as he rehearsed the speech, and he imagined that Carroll would respond affirmatively. But he recalled what George Jefferson had said to him on the subject. He was too young. He had best just leave it to the authorities. And the more rational part of his brain told him that Carroll would say the same thing, and then he would imagine going to see Judge Parker and delivering his speech. Someone, surely, would listen. But he had no way of traveling from Bentonville to Fort Smith, and besides that, when he tried to explain it all to his mother, she wouldn't hear of it. So Sam sat home and pouted. He rehearsed his speech again, and it made him cry again, and when his mother wasn't watching, he loaded the gun and sneaked out of the house. He walked a ways out of town, and he found some discarded cans and bottles and set them up as targets, and he shot at them. He missed more often than not. He was not a good shot with a handgun. But he kept shooting. He would get better.

Maletha Maples thought at times that her house was much too small for her and her six children. At other times, acutely conscious of the absence of her husband, it seemed somehow too big. It was not full. There was unoccupied space which should not be empty. At times she wondered if she would be able to make it without Dan. At other times she simply told herself that she would. Somehow she would. She had no choice. The oldest of her six was still just a boy at sixteen, although he didn't seem to think so. Sam thought he was grown. He thought that he should be able to do what he wanted to do, make his own decisions, go his own ways. And, of course, what Sam had been put through in Tahlequah had aged him in some ways, real fast and unnatural. She was worried more about Sam than about anything else, and she certainly had plenty to worry over. How could she make a decent living without a husband? She had never before had to earn money. How would she do that now? Could she earn enough for a family of seven? And even if she could manage to earn the money, how would she be able to raise her children properly while working for a living? They all needed her attention, the youngest because they were yet so young, and the oldest because— because they too were yet so young. The times were so difficult for them. They all needed her now more than ever before, yet for the first time in their short lives, she was not going to be able to be there for them. She would have to work. She would have to work at something.

But Sam worried her most of all. He had been there, had seen the shooting, had sat in the room with his dying father. What must it have been like for Sam, she wondered, and she knew that she could not begin to imagine. What had it done to him? He was only sixteen years old. Just a boy. He had practically worshipped his father. He had believed that Dan was all powerful and all knowing, could do no wrong and could come to no harm. And he had been forced to watch him die and at such a tender age. Now he had turned sullen and sulky, and he had kept Dan's gun. Every chance he got, he sneaked off to shoot. She knew he was doing that, even though he thought that it was his secret. She knew where he was going and she knew why. He had begged her to let him go to Fort Smith to try to join up with the deputies there. When she had refused, he had said that he would go anyway. Finally she had said to him, "Well, I guess I can't stop you," and maybe that had been the right thing to say, because he was still at home, still pouting, still sneaking off to shoot. Losing Dan had been a terrible thing for Maletha, a thing that she had thought she couldn't survive, but this, she thought, was even worse. She was afraid, dreadfully afraid, that she was losing Sam, her first-born, in an even more sinister way, and she had no idea what to do about it. She did not know how to expunge bitterness from the heart and soul of a child.

Chapter 7

Ned Christie's life went on as usual. Friends and relatives came to visit. Ned and his family went to visit friends and relatives. They worked their garden and they gathered wild foods in season. They tended their animals. They hunted. Ned's customers, most of whom were also friends and relatives, brought him their business. So life went on as usual. But there were new topics of conversation. Had Isaac Parker, "the Hanging Judge," bothered to answer Ned's letter? No. Of course not. Who had seen federal lawmen most recently? Where had they seen them? And there was still the old talk about the allotment of Cherokee lands, the plans of the United States government for taking over Cherokee lands and making each individual Cherokee a private landowner. Ned Christie always spoke out strongly against allotment and against the enrollment process that had to be accomplished first.

"They can't give you an allotment," he would say,

"if they don't have your name on their list. Don't sign up."

The traditional Cherokee mind could not conceive of private ownership of land, but it well knew that white men engaged in such a practice.

"They want to turn us into white men," Ned would say.

And there was more. This allotment business had another side, which Ned and other thoughtful Cherokees could see. If the United States gave each Cherokee his private farm, and if they multiplied the number of acres in each farm by the number of newly made Cherokee landowners, they would find that there were thousands and thousands of acres of Cherokee land left over. The United States would take that land for whites.

"And it would mean the end of our government," he would tell them. "If we let them do this, there will be no more Cherokee Nation. They want to make themselves another state, and they want to make it at our expense, out of our land."

Ned Christie had been declared an outlaw, and so he no longer went to Tahlequah to the capital to make his speeches. But many went to him to hear the things he had to say. So life went on for Ned Christie, but the lives of his neighbors changed. Ned Christie did not ask them to change their lives, nor did they ask for his opinion on the matter. They simply took it on themselves to do what they knew needed to be done. When they went to town, they listened for the news. When they saw strangers in the neighborhood, they watched. And Ned Christie's life went on as usual.

But none of them were prepared for what Heck Thomas was planning.

Heck Thomas had gathered his force. He had Isbel, of course. Isbel's home was Vinita, a town in the Cherokee Nation for which Ned Christie had no love. Vinita represented another battle lost by the Cherokees, for Vinita was a railroad town. It would not have existed at all had the conservative Cherokees succeeded in their efforts to keep the railroad out of the Cherokee Nation, but the railroad interests had won that fight, and the railroad had come through. It had created new towns, and it had brought more people into the Cherokee Nation. More non-citizens. White people. It had been a political fight, fought in the legislative sessions of the Cherokee Nation and in the halls of the United States Congress. It had been fought by businessmen and politicians and lobbyists in boardrooms and in secret meetings and with shady deals and with payoffs. Isbel was from Vinita, and he was familiar with the Cherokee Nation. He would lead Thomas and the other three men to Ned Christie's house.

"I can get us out there after dark," said Isbel, "and I can locate five different places around the Christie home. One for each of us. Well out. We'll be moving in on him from five different directions. We'll each be about the same distance away from the house, so we should all get there about the same time."

"Can we time it to get there just about daybreak?" asked Thomas.

"Yeah. Sure," said Isbel. "That's what I was thinking, too."

"You know this territory," said Thomas. "You'll know where you're going out there. The rest of us don't. Is there a chance we might get lost out in them woods after dark?"

"I don't think so," said Isbel. "I can give you pretty good directions. It ought to work."

Then Isbel drew a map, and the five men studied it and went over their plans again. They would get Ned Christie.

It was slow going in the dark through the thick woods on the rocky, uneven ground, and Heck Thomas wondered more than once if he really knew where he was going. There was a ridge just to his left, however, and Isbel had told him that if he just kept it there, it would lead him right to Ned Christie's house. Thomas couldn't always see the ridge, but if he wandered off to his left, he encountered the sharp rise. He wondered if the other three men were doing as well as he. Isbel, of course, would know right where he was going. A whole lot depended on Isbel's knowledge and on Isbel's planning and timing. Thomas didn't particularly like having to depend so much on another man's brain, but he really hadn't had much choice in this case.

He noticed that he could see a little better. The sun was coming up somewhere. He couldn't see it in the deep woods, but he could tell that it was getting lighter. He was seeing better. After that it seemed as if the light increased at a steady, though slow, rate of speed. And then he saw a clearing up ahead. He was coming to the edge of the woods. Isbel's timing had been damn near perfect, if only the other four were arriving at their appointed places at the same time. He stopped for a moment, looking around himself, but looking mainly toward the clearing. Ned Christie's house, he knew, should be right up there ahead. Thomas should be approaching the house from the west, or from its left side. The shop should be between him and the house. He would move through the woods just a little to his own left in order to gain a view of the front door of the house. Somewhere farther to his left, approaching from the far side of the ridge, Isbel should be there facing directly the front of the house. A third man should be coming in from the east, way on the other side of the clearing, almost directly opposite Thomas. The three of them would have the front of the house covered, from directly in front, from the right, and from the left. The other two men would approach from behind the house.

Everyone had been instructed to wait for Heck Thomas. He might shout out an order to surrender, or he might shoot. At any rate, no one else was to be the first to make a move. The sun was still low, but it was light. All five men, Thomas thought, should be in place. He wished for a way to be sure of that, but of course there was no way. He would just have to trust that everything had worked out according to plan. He moved slowly and cautiously a little closer to the edge of the woods, and then he saw the house. It was just as Isbel had described it.

The clearing was mostly a valley, and Ned Christie's house and shop were built up on the hill on the south side overlooking the valley below. The ridge that Thomas had used as his guide through the woods in the dark became the hill on the valley's north. Thomas took a hard look at the house. Then he moved again. He wanted to see if he could spot Isbel before he gave himself away. He would take his chances on the other three being in place, but he didn't want to start anything without Isbel's being there. He stepped up behind a tall and thick red oak tree, and he saw Isbel move in the woods far to his left. He was in place. But just at that same instant, the dogs began to bark.

"Damn," said Thomas.

They had been discovered.

Inside the cabin, Ned Christie had just poured himself a cup of coffee. He was about to sit down at the table when he heard the dogs. He put the cup down on the table and moved to the front door. His Winchester rifle was standing there beside the door, loaded and ready. He picked it up and looked over his shoulder at Arch and Gatey. Arch was still sleepy-eyed. Gatey was mixing dough for bread in a large bowl. Both of them stood still and returned Ned's steady gaze. Outside the dogs still barked. Ned's left hand went to the door.

"*Nede,*" said Gatey.

Ned looked back at his wife.

"Don't open the door," she said. "Look out first."

He hesitated a moment, then walked over to the ladder that led up to the loft. He climbed the ladder, taking the Winchester with him, and he crouched low, moving over to the window. Being careful not to expose himself, he looked outside. He could see the old spotted hound barking, and he looked where the dog was looking. He waited patiently for a long moment. Then he saw a slight movement, almost imperceptible. At first he could tell no more. He waited, and then he saw it again. Straight out in front of the house, across the valley clearing on the edge of the woods, there was a man there behind a tree with a rifle in his hands. Ned spoke in a low voice, just loud enough so that Gatey and Arch could hear.

"There's someone out there," he said.

"Laws?" said Arch.

"Most likely," said Ned. "I can't tell. He's hiding in the woods."

"Just one?" said Gatey.

"I only see one. There's probably more."

Slowly he raised the window sash. The glass windowpanes were among several luxuries the log home boasted and were sources of special pride to the Christies. But they were difficult to ease up without attracting attention. He got the window up about a foot, and then he moved around to get a better angle for himself. He poked the barrel of the Winchester out the window in the general direction of the hiding man, not yet taking aim.

Heck Thomas, from his spot behind the oak, saw the rifle barrel. He could see that it was pointed toward Isbel, and he figured that the man in the house, probably Ned Christie, had not seen him, had seen only Isbel. He raised his own rifle and fired. Isbel fired an instant later.

Ned Christie ducked back from the window as shards of shattered window glass flew around him.

"Two," he said.

With his rifle he knocked out the rest of the window and ducked away again as two more shots were fired at him from the woods. He needed to know the location of the second man. He could tell from the shots that the man was off somewhere to his own left. He didn't know how far left. He popped back up into the window and fired a quick shot straight ahead, but he looked to his left. As the man out front ducked behind his cover tree, the man to the far left stepped out from behind his to fire at Ned. Ned spotted him and pulled back just in time. The bullet thudded into the window frame.

Ned moved again. This time he fired quickly, two shots at the man on the left, two straight ahead. Then he ducked back out of the way, and return fire came hard and fast from both directions.

Heck Thomas yelped in spite of himself when bits of bark stung the side of his face as Ned Christie's bullet struck the tree much too close for comfort. It felt as if he had been sprayed by a dozen or so tiny nettles. That was almost a hell of a shot, he said to himself. He began to fall back into the woods, watching the cabin's loft window carefully as he moved from tree to tree. When he felt like he had moved back far enough into the woods for safety, he started moving his way toward Isbel. He had not expected Ned Christie to be this much trouble. He had heard of Cherokees accused of murder surrendering without a fight, without even a protest, and he had heard of others, convicted and condemned to die by their own tribal courts and having been allowed to go home on their own recognizance to set their affairs in order, returning voluntarily on the appointed day to be executed. He had expected, at most, a token resistance from Ned Christie, and already he had been met by far more than that.

He heard a movement in the woods just ahead, and he ducked behind a tree, rifle ready. Then he heard a voice.

"Heck? That you?"

"Yeah," said Thomas. He stepped out and moved ahead to join Isbel, who had also retreated.

"What do we do now?" said Isbel.

"We have to get him out of that house some way," said Thomas. "That son of a bitch shoots fast and straight."

"What's he shooting at us with anyway?" said Isbel.

"I'd say a .44–40," said Thomas. "Probably a Winchester. Goddamn thing holds eighteen rounds."

"He's shot five, I think."

"Likely reloaded by now."

There was a rustling in the woods behind Isbel,

and Thomas jerked his rifle up ready for action.

"What's that?" he said in a harsh whisper.

In answer to his question, the other three posse members appeared.

"What's going on?" said the one in the lead. "We heard shots. Then nothing."

"Why aren't you watching the back of the house?" said Thomas.

"There's no way out the back," said the accused deputy. "No door. No windows. We thought you might need us around here."

"Okay," said Thomas. "Let's spread out just a little here, and move back up to the edge of the trees. He's in the loft. Watch out. He's a sharpshooter. Maybe the five of us together can drive him out of there. Let's go."

They fanned out, and they crouched low, and they darted from tree to tree. Soon they were in their new positions ready to renew the onslaught. Each man took a bead on the loft window, and each man waited. The other four waited for Heck Thomas to begin.

During the lull, Ned Christie had reloaded his Winchester. He had also called to Arch to bring him his revolvers, two Model 1861 Colt .44 cap and ball pistols, which Ned's father, Watt, had carried during the Civil War. Ned had retooled the pistols to fire cartridges, along the lines of the Richards conversion system, used by the United States Army. Arch checked the revolvers to see that they were loaded, then climbed up the ladder far enough to hand them to his father. Ned put the Colts on the loft floor there beneath the window. They would not be as useful as the Winchester because of the range across the valley clearing. They were there for backup, just in case he might need them.

"Are they gone?" asked Arch.

"I don't know," said Ned. He put his face in the window for an instant and then drew back quickly.

Heck Thomas saw the motion in the window and fired. Four other rifles echoed that first shot. At least fifteen shots were fired before Thomas managed to relay a cease-fire command.

"Did we get him?" someone asked.

Ned Christie moved to the window with his Winchester and fired as rapidly as he could. His quick fire caused all five deputies to hug the far sides of the trees they were using for cover. When Ned had fired the last bullet from the Winchester, he tossed the rifle to Arch.

"Load it," he said, and he picked up the Colts, one in each hand, and he fired one more round out the window. He wanted to make sure that the deputies knew that he could still shoot. They might have been counting his shots. Arch was busy shoving cartridges into the loading gate on the right side of the Winchester's receiver.

"Fall back," said Heck Thomas. "Fall back."

Once more Thomas moved back a safe distance

into the woods. This time he gathered his posse around him.

"We're getting nowhere, Heck," said Isbel.

"Listen," said Thomas. "I'm going to work my way back through the woods around to the right. I'm going to get as close to that shop there as I can. When I come out of the trees, I want you four to open up on that window. You got that?"

"What are you going to do?" asked Isbel.

"I'm going to set that shop on fire," said Thomas. "That's the man's business there, his livelihood. I expect he'll try to save it. Even if I'm wrong, the fire will get on over to the house eventually, don't you think?"

"Yeah," said Isbel. "They're set pretty close together."

"All right," said Thomas. "You all move back into position. When you see me run for the shop, open up."

Chapter 8

Ned was worried about what the posse might be up to. They had been silent again for a time. All three of his weapons were fully loaded, and, with the Winchester in his hands, he eased back into the window for a look. They were still out there, straight across the valley clearing from the house. He could see them there, huddled behind trees. There were two, three of them. No. There was a fourth. Four men straight out front. They were waiting for something. On the main floor of the cabin, Arch, his curiosity about to get the best of him, headed for a window to look outside.

"No," said Gatey. "Stay away from there."

"But what are they doing out there?" said Arch.

"They seem to be just waiting," said Ned, "but they're up to something."

Then he saw the man off to his left, a fifth man, run from the trees, running across a small piece of the clearing, racing toward the shop. Ned raised the

Winchester to his shoulder, but the four men straight ahead started shooting, and he had to duck back to avoid being shot to pieces.

Heck Thomas threw himself to the ground at the west end of the shop. He had made it. The cover fire had worked. The shop was between him and the house, and there was no way Ned Christie could see him from up in the loft in the house. The rapid fire from the deputies continued as Thomas tried to get back his breath. It had only been a short run, but he was gasping for air, and his chest was pounding. He looked around. There were plenty of dry leaves and twigs and sticks well within his reach. He scraped up a pile of the stuff, shoving it against the wall of the shop. He felt in his shirt pockets for matches, located them and pulled one out. His fingers were trembling, causing him to fumble with the match, and the slight breeze blew the flame out as soon as he had struck it. He found a second match and tried to calm himself. He planned more carefully, struck the match and cupped the flame in his hands. Then he lit the pile of woods debris. The flame was slow in starting, and Thomas nurtured it, sheltered it with his body and with his hands, blew on it a little, fed it small, dry twigs. At last it began to move on its own. It began to grow. Still Thomas fed it, nursed it, coaxed it toward the wall of the shop. The flames grew, and they crackled as they licked the wall. Thomas stood up and looked around himself. The shots continued, but they were not as close together as before. He saw some old boards lying on the ground a few feet away, and he picked them up and leaned them against the shop's wall, forming a kind of shed over the fire. Soon the flames were lapping their way up the diagonal path of the boards and higher up the wall of the shop. Satisfied at last, Thomas looked back toward the trees.

He took a deep breath, and he ran, and a bullet from the loft nicked at his heels, but the barrage from the woods once more increased, and he ran harder, faster, and he reached the cover of the trees. He had not been hit. He made his way back to where the others waited for him, and as he moved through the woods, he glanced now and again toward the shop, and he saw with satisfaction the flames leaping higher and higher.

"Nede," said Gatey, "your shop is on fire."

Ned knew that flames from the shop would soon leap on over to the house. He knew that they were no longer safe in the house. He should have killed that man, he thought. He could have, had he tried a little harder. But Ned had hoped that somehow Judge Parker might yet come around before things had gone too far. He had not wanted to kill any of these men. He had thought, even as they were trying to kill him, as they were shooting bullets into his home from their hiding places behind the trees, he had thought even then that he could just drive them away, and that everything might yet be worked out satisfactorily. He had not wanted war with the United States, not a shooting war. A shooting war could not be won. But now they had set fire to his shop, and soon the house would be ablaze. They meant to drive him out into the open, where he would either be forced to surrender, or where he would present an easy target. Well, he would not give up. He would not be taken like a common criminal to Fort Smith to the court of Isaac Parker.

"We have to get out," he said. He fired two quick shots at the deputies, then took up the Colts and tucked them in the waistband of his trousers. Carrying the rifle, he climbed down from the loft as bullets from the posse's rifles whizzed through the window above. They would have to leave by the front door, stepping right out into the line of fire, but the safety of the woods was just around the corner, behind the house. Ned gave hurried instructions, then flung open the door and stepped outside. He fired at the posse as Gatey came out the front door behind him and ran to the right heading for the trees behind the house. Flames from the shop had vaulted over to the house, and Ned could feel the heat on his back and hear the loud pops and the crackling behind him. As bullets flew around him, Ned cranked the Winchester and fired back. Arch ran after his mother.

The deputies were suddenly confused. One had fallen back to a safer distance in the trees, and two fired shots after the fleeing Arch. None of them hit their marks. Isbel reached around his protective tree to try to draw a deadly bead on Ned Christie, but in doing so, he exposed too much of himself at the wrong time. Ned sent a .44–40 slug crashing into Isbel's right shoulder.

"Ah."

Isbel screamed and dropped his rifle. His right arm fell uselessly to his side, and blood spurted from the wound. A second later, Heck Thomas fired at Ned. Ned felt a sudden explosion in his head, and all he could see at first was the color of blood. He roared out a mixture of pain, surprise, and anger, and he dropped his Winchester. Both hands went up instinctively, and he could feel the warm, sticky blood all over his face. He did not know where he had been hit. His whole face hurt. His whole face felt bloody, raw, mushy. Intense pain followed the initial shock, and Ned fell to his knees. All he could see was blackness, and from an indefinite distance, a seeming infinity, a tiny dot of red appeared. The red dot was moving at incredible speed, heading straight for his face. It came closer and closer, growing larger and larger, until it took over his whole field of vision. Everything that had been black was red, and then the red exploded or diffused, and all was black again save the tiny red dot in the distance that was moving toward him again.

Arch was about to go into the woods when he glanced back over his shoulder and saw his father on his knees and saw the blood.

"Mom," he shouted, and he ran back for Ned. The posse had stopped shooting. Isbel was out of commission. Heck Thomas apparently thought that his last shot had done the job. He had lowered his rifle. The other three deputies were hidden. Arch ran up beside Ned, and Gatey came right behind him. She grabbed Ned by an arm and pulled.

"Come on," she said. "Come on."

While Gatey pulled Ned to his feet and started
leading him toward the trees, Arch grabbed up the
Winchester. He quickly chambered a round, and he
raised the rifle to his shoulder and snapped it off at
Thomas. The bullet grazed the top of Thomas's ear
and scratched some skin from the side of his skull.

"Ow. Damn," he shouted, and he ran for cover.

"Heck," shouted a deputy. "Isbel's hurt bad."

Thomas glanced in Isbel's direction; then back toward Arch. Arch was no longer standing there before
the blazing house. He was about to disappear into
the woods. Thomas sent a wild shot in his direction,
and Arch turned to fire back once more. A second
shot from Thomas struck him in the chest. He stood
for a moment, stunned. He did not drop the rifle,
neither did he raise it. He turned slowly and walked
into the woods.

Heck Thomas ran to the spot where Isbel sat leaning
back against a tree. Isbel's right shoulder, arm and
side were blood-soaked, and the blood was still running freely from the wound in the shoulder. Thomas
looked at Isbel. Isbel stared straight ahead. He did
not appear to see. He must have been in shock. Thomas shot a glance at the deputy standing nearest to
Isbel.

"You stay with him," he said. "Do what you can.
We're going after Ned Christie."

The other two followed Thomas. They ran across
the valley clearing to the house, which was still in
flames.

"They're both hurt," said Thomas. "They can't

get far. Two shot men and a woman. They went in right over here. Let's go get them. Be careful."

They went into the woods behind the house on the Christies' trail, but they could find no sign of any of the three. For some minutes, they looked in vain. Then Heck Thomas called it off.

"We got to get Isbel to a doctor," he said, "before he bleeds to death. Let's get out of here. Damn it, I'd like to have found them two, but I don't believe that either one of them will live, the way they was shot. Come on. Let's get the horses and get back to town."

Gatey led her husband and her son through the woods. Behind her, her house and all her possessions were burning to ashes, but she did not look back. She did not think about the house nor about the things it held. The past was gone, even the very recent past, and the present was all important. On her right hand was her husband, who had been shot. On her left hand was her only son, also shot. She led them through the woods. They needed care, even such as she could give until a doctor could be found, but first they needed safety. The white man's laws were just behind them in the woods. She knew they were in pain and they were losing precious blood, but she knew as well that they could not afford to stop. They had to get away. She didn't look at them unless she had to. She looked straight ahead. She looked where she was going. She looked the way she was leading them.

The woods were thick, and as they went deeper

into them, they got even thicker. Gatey had to watch
for tangles on the ground, vines and brambles which
might trip them up or snare a foot. She had to watch
for low-hanging branches. She had to dodge these
things herself, and she had to help both Ned and
Arch to dodge them, too. The trees were close together, and she had to weave her way, and Ned's,
and Arch's way, between them. And the ground was
rocky and uneven and cluttered with deadfall from
the trees. With each step there was danger of stub-
bing a toe on a rock or stumbling over a fallen
branch or stepping in a hole and spraining an ankle
or breaking a bone. She had to watch for all of that.
She had to watch it for herself, and she had to watch
it for Ned and for Arch.

And yet she had to hurry. She knew that time was
a luxury that she could not afford. The white man's
laws were back there, and they had to get away. The
wounds were bleeding, and they needed tending.
They had to keep moving. They had to go fast. They
could not afford to slow down.

Arch was conscious of walking fast, walking behind his mother. He was cognizant somehow of the
fact that his mother was now in charge. But he was
in a daze, a spell. His eyes were wide, and his face
wore a stunned expression. He felt no pain. He only
felt the uneven earth beneath his feet, the weight of
the Winchester in his hands, the sense of urgency in
the pace his mother set for them, and the cold wind
whistling in the hole in his chest. And he was conscious of a single thought: He had to follow his

mother, he had to keep up with his mother, he had
to do what Mother said, or die.

Ned Christie stumbled in frightening darkness
over the rough and treacherous breast of the earth.
He was like a child. No. Worse than a child. He
could not see. Each step he took brought new un-
certainties. Was the ground ahead a two-foot drop?
Was it as high as his waist? Was it perilous with
slippery rocks or dry and flat and hard? Or would
his next step send him plunging into a deep and dark
abyss? A hand pulled him along by his sleeve, sometimes shoved him this way or that. His wife's hand?
He thought so. But he could not see. He saw black,
and he saw red, but he saw no shapes, no shadows,
no outlines, only swirling black and red.

And there was the fear of what was following.
The deputy marshals would be on his trail. They had
shot him once, but he was not yet dead, so they were
back there. They'd be coming. How many were
they? Five? But he had shot one, hadn't he? Then
there were four. Four armed lawmen coming up behind, and he was blind. He could not see. He knew
he had his pistols in his belt, for he could feel them
with each step, and they were loaded too, he thought.
But he had lost his rifle. The pistols, then, would
have to do. Watt's pistols. But where were the lawmen? He could not see.

He felt small branches lash at him in the darkness
as Gatey led him stumbling this way and that. And
there was the pain. It was like the pain of a thousand
hangovers all at once, a thousand hangovers from
the cheapest bootleg whiskey. He felt as if his head

had been split open. And when he touched his face with his hand, he thought his face was one large scab, and his nose was like a mushroom, flat and wide and tender to the touch.

But where was Arch?

He didn't know. He wanted to ask, but something kept his voice still. His face, perhaps, simply did not dare to move. But there was something more. It was an undefinable compulsion that drove him forward through the darkness and told him not to hesitate for anything, to keep moving, to keep breathing, to go where he was guided by the hand that he thought was his wife's. But what had become of his son?

Through the fear and the pain and the urgency to move, he thought about some things. He thought about the unjust accusation, the false charge that he had killed a man. And then he thought about his letter to the judge, the arrogant judge who had refused to respond. The judge had responded though. He had responded with those five men, and his first word had been a gunshot. He reminded himself that he had tried to do things right. A Cherokee who would go to Parker's court would have to be a fool, but Ned had written his request and offered to prove that he was innocent of the charge. Then he had received Parker's answer in the form of a five-man posse that shot first with no warning given. Even then he had not tried to kill them. He had thought to just drive them away. But they had kept shooting into his home, they had burned his shop and his house, they had shot him in the face and blinded him, and now they pursued him through these blackened woods, through this strange and hostile darkness. Ah. Where was Arch?

Well, they had forced it. They had gone too far. The decision had been taken out of his hands. Now there would be no turning back. Now it was war, war with the federal lawmen. It was Ned Christie's War.

"Hla Gilisi yijiwonisgesdi," he muttered.

He made the sounds almost without thinking, almost before realizing that he had spoken. He had formed the words painfully, through thick and swollen lips caked and dried with blood.

"What?" said Gatey. "What did you say?"

And so he said it one more time.

"I will never speak English again."

Gatey got Ned and Arch safely to the cave. She had known all along exactly where she was going. She would have gotten there sooner, much sooner, had she chosen to cross the clearing. Because of the posse, she had taken the longer way, through the woods. She took them both inside and lay them down. It was dark inside the cave, and cool and damp. There were so many things to be done, and Gatey had to keep her head. She needed water with which to bathe the wounds, cold water from the creek outside. She had nothing in which to carry water. She would take off her apron and soak it in the creek. It would probably take several trips, but it would work. It would have to do. She calmed and settled Ned and Arch as much as possible, and then she went outside. The creek ran near the mouth of the cave, so she was soon at the water's edge, bending over to soak the apron. She heard a sound behind her. She jumped, startled, and turned.

"Gatey. I heard shooting."

Gatey gasped, then recovered herself quickly. It was Young Archie Wolf, a neighbor.

"It was the laws," she said. "They shot Ned and Arch. I hid them in the cave up there."

"How can I help?" said Archie Wolf.

"I need a fire built in the cave," said Gatey.

While Gatey bathed the wounds of Ned and Arch, Young Wolf built a small fire inside the cave. It would take the dampness and the chill out of the air, and it would provide some light.

"What now?" he said.

"I don't know if they're still out there," she said.

"I'll go and look."

"Wait," she said. She took up the Winchester that lay on the floor of the cave beside her son, and she held it out toward Archie Wolf. "Take this," she added.

He grabbed the rifle and left the cave. Gatey continued working on the wounds. She made another trip down to the creek to rinse and resoak the apron, and then she went back into the cave. Ned's face wound had stopped bleeding, but blood still seeped from the hole in Arch's chest. She concentrated on that one. Cold water should stop the bleeding. Soon Young Archie Wolf returned.

"They're gone," he said, and he leaned the rifle against the wall of the cave. "I'll go and get my father."

Old Wolf was an Indian doctor, well known and highly respected. He was also a close neighbor and a cherished friend. When he at last arrived at the cave, carrying with him his bag of herbs and medical paraphernalia, Gatey felt a sense of relief and hope. The gunshot wounds were bad, but she had faith in the knowledge, skills, and medicine of Old Wolf. If anything could be done, he was the man who could do it. The old man looked at Ned, and he looked at Arch. The chest wound, he decided, required the most immediate care. He spoke to his son, Archie Wolf, in a low voice, and Archie reached into the old man's bag. He withdrew a short clay pipe, some tobacco, some sprigs of cedar, and a few matches. Then he gave the pipe, tobacco, and some of the matches to Gatey.

"He says that you should smoke this," he told her, "just outside the cave."

Gatey stepped out just beyond the entrance, and she found there a flat, smooth rock. She used it for a chair, sitting down and filling the pipe bowl. She struck the match and lit the tobacco, puffing on the pipe. Watching the blue-gray smoke rise up and dissipate in the sky, she knew that Old Wolf was at work, and she knew that somehow she was involved in the process. She was helping. Inside the cave, Young Wolf was lighting sprigs of cedar here and there.

So Gatey smoked. By and by Young Wolf came out and sat beside her.

"Arch's wound is clean, I think," he said. "He should be all right. He'll heal."

"And Ned?" asked Gatey.

"He'll live, I think," said Wolf. "My father showed me the wound. It's bad, but it's not nearly so bad as it might have been. The bullet hit the bridge of his nose. His nose is broken. Then it tore his eye, his right eye. The eye is no good anymore. It can't be fixed. The bullet stayed under the skin and went around his head. It's at the back of his skull now still under the skin. Father will take it out of there. I've never heard of a gunshot wound like that before. Never."

They could hear the soft voice of Old Wolf inside the cave. He might have been singing. They couldn't tell for sure.

Off to the right of Young Archie Wolf, a dung beetle diligently rolled its idiosyncratic acquisition towards its home. No one noticed the tiny creature at its hard labor. The powers of the universe gave no indication of awareness, much less interest in its life and its task. And certainly the two human beings sitting nearby did not. Yet it moved forward with determination, pushing along ahead of itself the nearly perfect sphere of fecal matter so necessary to its short and obscure life. It moved steadily forward, heading east, going uphill, a long, steady climb, considering the beetle's size. It was a straight and steady climb, until the sharp ridge of rock arose in its path. It was a rise running more or less north and south, one that would hardly have been noticed by a larger creature, but it absolutely halted the progress of the beetle. The ball stopped rolling. The beetle pushed and strained. Suddenly the ball shot sideways and rolled away to the west. The beetle turned around several times, confused.

Inside the cave, the soft singing voice of Old Wolf, if it really had been singing, came to a stop. Young Archie stood up and went inside. A moment later he returned to Gatey's side.

"I'm going to get some food," he said, "and some more help. I won't be long."

Young Archie did return and did bring food, and Old Wolf prepared for Ned and Arch Christie some sweating tea to drink. He gave instructions to Gatey for their care, and he promised to come back from time to time. And others came, friends and neighbors and relatives from all around the countryside. They brought food and clothes, and some brought bullets for Ned's guns. They stocked the cave until it had become a home. And just in case the deputies came back, Young Wolf assured Gatey, there were people out watching all the possible ways in. No one could get near without being seen, and if someone was spotted coming in, the people could get back to the cave with warnings well ahead of the invaders.

"Still," he said, "they'll keep coming, and if they get this far and find this cave, you'll have to be ready to defend it."

Young Wolf and other men went out to look around. Where, they asked, would be the best place to make a stand in case a posse came on through? At last they decided. The best place would be the

cave itself, or very near the cave. The opening of
the cave was at the dead end of a kind of natural
path that ran uphill from the creek. On each side of
the natural path was a hogback or escarpment, so
that the path, in effect, was walled. Where it began
at the water's edge, the path was wide enough for
half a dozen men to walk along it side by side, but
by the time it reached the mouth of the cave, it had
narrowed, so that only two could do so comfortably.
At the same time, as the path moved uphill, closer
to the cave, the distance from the path up to the
escarpments' ledges decreased.

Young Wolf suggested a breastworks, a wall of
stone, across the path, about one-third of the distance
down from the mouth of the cave.

"But that would block Gatey's way to the water,"
said Marvin Pumpkin.

"No," said Gatey, having overheard. "That sounds
like a good plan. I can go out that way."

She pointed to the right-hand side of the path just
at the entrance to the cave. The ledge was lower
there, and the way to the top was not so steep. And
so the decision was made, and under the direction
of Young Archie Wolf, the work on the wall was
begun.

Chapter 9

Four men had congregated in the yard in front of the capitol in Tahlequah. They sat on a bench there facing the street, and while the traffic moved up and down in front of them, they talked. One man held a twig in his left hand and shaved it with a penknife in his right. Another chewed tobacco. A third was smoking a corncob pipe. A fourth just sat with his hands tucked inside his overall bib. The leaves were falling from the big trees in the yard behind them, and the four men talked in Cherokee.

"Were you here when the posse came back to town?" said one.

"I was here," said another. "I was sitting right here, and Peacheater was hear, too. We were just sitting here, talking, just like we are right now."

"That's right," said Peacheater, the man with the pipe. "What Cabbagehead says is right. We were right here, and they came in from the east, but we could see them. Who else was here that day?"

"Oh, let's see," said Cabbagehead. "I think that *Edohi* was here."

"Joe Walker? That half-breed?" said the whittler.

"Yeah," said Peacheater. "That one. He was here with us. Anyway, like I said, they came in from the east, and they stopped down there at the hotel because that one was hurt real bad."

"Isbel," said Cabbagehead. "He was shot. Ned Christie shot him."

"Yeah. Isbel," said Peacheater. "He lives over at Vinita, I think. A white man. Anyway, they took him in there, and then, I guess, they went to find Doc Blake. They didn't want an Indian doctor. They wanted a white man doctor, and Doc Blake's the only one around I guess."

"Doc Blake worked on Dan Maples," said the whittler. "Dan Maples died."

"Isbel wasn't shot up as bad as Maples," said Cabbagehead, "so he didn't die."

"He won't be riding out with a posse again any time real soon though," said Peacheater. "His shoulder's broke up pretty bad, I think. But Heck Thomas and the others came on down this way after they got Doc Blake to the hotel."

"They rode their horses right down the street here," said Cabbagehead.

"Heck Thomas said he thought he'd killed Ned Christie and Ned's boy Arch. He said he shot Arch right through the chest, and he shot Ned right in the face."

"That's what he said," said Cabbagehead. "I heard it, too."

"He said he didn't bring the bodies back because of Isbel. He said Ned and Arch ran away in the woods, and Isbel was bleeding too bad for him to take the time to find them."

"That's right," said Cabbagehead.

"But he said they couldn't live out there in the woods as bad as they were shot. He said they'll die. They burned his house down, too."

"Ned Christie's house," said Cabbagehead. "The posse burned it down."

"They didn't die," said the one with his hands under his overall bib, the one who had not spoken before.

"Have you seen Ned Christie?" said Cabbage-head.

The quiet one just nodded his head affirmatively.

"Well," said Peacheater, "Heck Thomas went on back to Fort Smith, I guess. He'll tell old Parker what he did out there."

"Maybe Parker will think Ned Christie's dead," said Cabbagehead. "Maybe they'll leave him alone now."

"Maybe," said Peacheater. "I don't know. I heard they shot his eye out."

"I heard that he swore that he'd never talk English again," said the whittler.

"That's not much," said the quiet one. "I don't like to talk English anyway."

"Ha," said Peacheater. "You don't even know any English."

"That's just because I don't want to talk it," said the other.

Isaac Parker stared out his office window toward the jail. It was a rainy day in Fort Smith, and the yard between the two buildings was fast turning into a mudhole. Parker looked with pride and satisfaction at the cement sidewalk that ran from one building to the other. People would appreciate that little accomplishment of his on a day like this. The joints in his hips were aching more than usual. He turned away from the window and walked back behind his desk. Each step was painful. He sat down in the big chair with a wince. Then he settled back to try to relax his tired old body. Marshal Carroll's letter of resignation lay there on his desk. The judge was waiting for Jacob Yoes, Carroll's replacement, to come in for an interview. There was one particular case he wanted to discuss. The papers for that case were there, too, spread out before him on the desk. He glanced at the warrant, now two years old, and at his notes.

Ned Christie. A full-blooded Cherokee Indian. A blacksmith and a gunsmith by trade. A member of the Cherokee Nation's legislative body (former). Educated. Fluent in both the English and the Cherokee languages. Description: 36 or 37 years of age. Tall and handsome by reports. Long hair that reaches halfway to his waist. A thin mustache and a sparse goatee. Facial features marred by gunshot wound that broke his nose and put out his right eye. (Shot fired by Dep. Heck Thomas.)

Shot and killed Dep. U.S. Marshal Daniel Maples on May 4, 1887. 1889 shot Dep. L.P. Isbel, crippling him for life. Dangerous. A deadly shot. A sworn enemy of the U.S. govt. His home is 12 miles east of Tahlequah.

He glanced up from the notes to see Jacob Yoes standing in his doorway.

"Ah, come in, Mr. Yoes," he said.

Yoes walked in, holding his hat in his hands. A big, thick-chested man, Yoes appeared to strain the seams of the suit he wore. Parker stood up and shook the marshal's hand. Then he indicated a chair.

"Sit down," he said, and he himself sat down again. He tried to hide his pain, to suppress the groans and winces that longed to break loose from inside him. "I've been wanting to talk to you, Mr. Yoes," he said.

"Yes, sir?" said Yoes.

"I know you've been busy," continued the judge, "and so have I, but I thought that we simply must make time for this discussion. You've heard of Ned Christie, Mr. Yoes?"

"Yes, I have," said Yoes. "He's the man who killed Dan Maples, isn't he?"

"Two years ago, Mr. Yoes," said Parker. "Two years. Two long years have gone by since that brutal, unprovoked murder. And Ned Christie is still at large. Still enjoying the comforts of home, the embraces of his wife. And Dan Maples, a good man, has lain in his cold grave for two years. Does that sound like justice to you, Mr. Yoes?"

"No, sir," said Yoes.

"This office is charged with the administration of justice. My job is to carry out that charge. Your job is to carry out that charge. The United States government depends on us. The Indian nations depend on us to deliver them from the hands of the lawless. What does it look like, Mr. Yoes, when the world knows that Ned Christie, a sworn enemy of the United States, has murdered an officer of the United States and continues to roam the countryside at will? After two long years? What does that look like?"

"Well, Your Honor," said Yoes, "I'd say that it looks pretty bad."

"Bad indeed," said Parker. "And what does it make us look like in the eyes of the world? You and me? This court?"

"I guess it makes us look like we can't do our job," said Yoes.

"It's a big job, Mr. Yoes," said Parker. "You know that, and I know it, but our critics do not know that, or they choose not to see it. Now, I know that you have a long list of fugitives to pursue and a vast area to patrol, but Mr. Yoes, I want you to make this Ned Christie case a matter of top priority. I want Ned Christie brought to justice, and that can mean that he is arrested and brought in for trial, or it can mean that his body is carried in."

"Yes, sir," said Yoes.

"But plan well, Mr. Yoes, and exercise extreme caution. Ned Christie is a dangerous man. The last posse to go after him was led by Deputy Marshal Heck Thomas. Do you know about that?"

"I've heard some stories, Your Honor," said Yoes.

"Heck Thomas and Larry Isbel," said Parker. "Two extremely able men. And they had three more with them. Ned Christie shot Isbel, crippling him for life. Ended his career. Ned Christie was severely wounded by Heck Thomas. Christie and his son. Heck told me that he expected them both to die of their wounds. Had Larry Isbel not been so seriously wounded, he would have pursued them to bring back the bodies.

"But Mr. Yoes, the Christies did not die. Word has come to me from the Cherokee Nation that both Christies have recovered fully from their wounds. We are the losers. Larry Isbel has not recovered. He's ruined for life. Dan Maples has been in his grave for two long years."

"Sir," said Yoes, "I'm in complete agreement with you. In fact, I've been studying the Ned Christie file in my office. I'd like to send Dave Rusk out there with a posse."

"Why Dave Rusk?" said Parker.

"Well, sir, Rusk lives in the Cherokee Nation. Up at Oaks. He owns a store over there. He does business with Cherokees. He even has a Cherokee employee, I believe. He knows the Cherokees. I think he'd be a good man for the job."

"So do I, Mr. Yoes," said Parker. "I just wanted to see what you would have to say about him. In fact, it was Dave Rusk who sent the word about Ned Christie to me, the word about his recovery. Go ahead, Mr. Yoes. Send Rusk."

———

The Christies continued to live in the cave while Ned
and Arch recuperated from the wounds received at
the hands of Heck Thomas. Ned was up and about
before Arch. His face had been disfigured by the
bullet from the deputy's gun, and his right eye had
been put out. Other than that, he was all right. His
friends had built the wall that Archie Wolf had pro-
posed, but so far it had not been needed. No lawmen
came. Ned, as soon as he could manage, began to
practice with his guns. The loss of his right eye had
affected his depth perception, and he found that he
had to start all over as a shootist. He made the ad-
justment, however, faster than he expected, and soon
he was shooting as well as ever before. But he did
not smile as much as before. He did not laugh at the
jokes his friends told. The scar across his face ran
deep. When Arch got up at last, he, too, wore on his
face an expression of gloom. Gatey tried for a time
to raise the spirits of her two men, but soon she, too,
was overcome by darkness. It was as if a dark pall
had been spread over the Christie home.

Friends still watched the roads, still brought supplies, but Ned was more concerned with bullets than
with food or clothing. In his spare time, which was
much, he shot. Then one day he noticed that Arch
was getting around much better.

"How is it, son?" he asked.

"Aw," said Arch. "I'm all right. Almost as good
as new. I'll be ready for them next time."

"Then let's go look at our house," said Ned.

———

Sam Maples was eighteen. He worked when he could find work, and most of his money he gave his mother to help with the younger children. But always he kept out some to use to buy bullets for his father's gun. He had kept the gun, and he kept the horse Dan Maples had owned. There had been hard times when his mother had insisted that they needed money more than they needed a horse and saddle. She had not, even then, dared to suggest that they sell the gun. But Sam always argued, and he had always won. She couldn't complain. He did work, and he did give her the money. Most of it. She knew that he bought bullets, and she knew that almost every day he rode the horse to someplace out of town to shoot. She knew that he still brooded over the loss of his father, and she knew that he still held deep within a strong desire for revenge. She didn't like it, but she had learned that there was nothing she could do. She told herself that she should count her blessings. He was a good son. He stayed at home, and he did give her most of his money.

Sam set the empty tin cans on top of fence posts, five of them. Then he stepped twenty-five paces away. His father's six-gun was strapped to his right hip, buckled around his waist, and tied down to his thigh. He turned and faced the posts, and then he pulled the revolver, drawing it up and out of the holster and cocking it with his thumb in one smooth move. He brought it out in front of himself at arm's length, pointed at a can and squeezed the trigger. The can went spinning off the post. He put the gun

back in the holster and went through the whole pro-
cedure again. Again he hit his target. He was getting
good. He knew. For the third shot, he simply swung
his arm to the right, cocked again, squeezed again.
Again his aim was true. He dropped his arm down
to his side, turned and walked away five steps, then
turned and fired again. This time he missed.

"Damn," he said. He fired again and hit his mark.
Reloading the revolver, the thought of his father's
hands, holding this same gun, putting bullets into
this same cylinder, thumbing back this same hammer, so many times it had been worn smooth. He
tried to picture his father, and he realized with a deep
sadness that he was losing the image. And so he held
on to the pistol. He strapped the same belt around
his waist. He climbed into the same old saddle and
listened to the same old leather creak. He rode the
same old tired horse and grew accustomed to its gait.
He listened to it pant and blow and neigh. In the
past year, he had noticed that his whiskers had begun
to grow. He let them grow above his lip, in spite of
the fact that his mustache was not very imposing,
but he shaved the rest of his face. He shaved it with
his father's razor, and he used his father's shaving
mug and brush. He even used the same old cake of
soap. He hadn't shaved enough to use that up. Recently he had tried on his father's boots, but those
were still too big. He wondered if he would grow
into them, or if, at eighteen, his growth was done.

He reloaded the revolver and holstered it. Then
he walked back to the fence, climbed it, and re-

trieved the cans. He tossed them over the fence, climbed back again, set them up again, and once again paced off his distance. This time he hit them all.

Chapter 10

They walked over to the old home site, the four of them: Ned Christie, Gatey, Arch Christie, and Young Archie Wolf. The first thing they saw was the cook-stove, standing alone in a pile of ashes. Not far away, the forge stood in the ash heap where the shop had been. The lower portion, the stone parts, of the two fireplaces still stood, but the chimneys had collapsed and burned. Other than that, everything on first glance gave the appearance of total loss. Ned walked into the gray ashes, and puffs of ash dust rose around his feet. Then he discovered that it was not, after all, a total loss. He found some items that could be salvaged: an iron pot, an iron skillet. They could be cleaned up and saved. He picked them up and tossed them out, away from the ash heap. Arch and Archie carried out the stove, and Ned wandered over to the ashes that had been his shop. There even more had survived. He brought out his 125-pound wrought-iron anvil with its steel face and long horn and heel. The double-speed, self-feed post drill was lying in the ashes, the post it had been attached to having been burnt to cinders. The drill, though, would be all right. It could be remounted. The forge would be all right, too, once its wooden handle was replaced. He found his screw plate with taps and dies and tap wrench, his sixty-pound vise, bolt clippers, farrier's pincers, nail-cutting nippers, hoof parers, rasp, farrier's knife, and toe knife. The hot and cold chisels, farrier's tongs, flat tongs, and bolt tongs were all okay. He would have to make new handles for all the hammers: the three-pound hand hammer, the ten-pound sledge, the eighteen-ounce farrier's hammer, the nine-ounce riveting hammer, and the two-pound ball-peen hammer. There were other salvageable items from both the house and the shop, more, in fact, than any of them had expected. They had approached the ashes with the feeling of complete loss, and therefore they had been pleasantly surprised at the number of things that had actually survived the conflagration. All those things, of course, would have to be cleaned up, but at least they had something. They had not been totally wiped out.

Ned turned and faced across the valley clearing, across the garden plot and the marble yard below. He was looking toward the spot at the edge of the woods where Isbel had been hiding when Ned had fired the shot that had broken the deputy's shoulder the day of the big fight, the day he had lost his eye.

"We'll rebuild over there," he said.

They spent the rest of that day cleaning up the

things they had salvaged from the fire. The next day was spent sharpening axes and saws and making new handles for axes and hammers. The third day the salvage was carried across the clearing, and a crude, lean-to shelter was built, under which to store all those things.

"Tomorrow," said Ned, "we'll start cutting trees."

They wandered through the woods, looking for just the right trees to cut, and when they found one, they cut it down with saws and axes, trimmed it, and tied it to the horse to be dragged out of the woods to the building site. Friends showed up to help. It was hard work and it was tedious, but slowly, over the days, the logs piled up. At last Ned was ready to start building, and with the advice of Old Wolf, a certain day was decided on for friends and neighbors to show up in the evening, after dark, to lay the worm rail, the first log of the new house, by the light of the moon. They would do no more work that night, but early the next morning, they would start building in earnest.

With shovels and hoes they leveled a place for the foundation, and on the appointed evening, under a bright, full moon, they laid the worm rail, a log that had been carefully prepared, squared off by hand by Ned Christie, for that purpose. The next day they started early. They would not erect a simple log cabin. This was to be a good-sized, solid home. And, though he did not tell anyone else his exact plans, Ned Christie's intentions were that it would be much more even than that. He did manage to let his friends

know about the things that he needed. He wanted
the logs to be all squared, and that would be much
more easily and quickly accomplished by the use of
a sawmill. And he wanted several loads of sand, lots
of sand. He hadn't asked anyone to do anything
about any of this. He had simply let his desires be
known.

The foundation had been laid, and numerous logs
had been cut. Everyone knew the morning was
planned to begin putting up the walls. Gatey had
boiled lots of coffee, and the men were having some
of that before starting to work. Ned noticed that
Young Archie Wolf was not present. He didn't say
anything to anyone though. Just a few feet away
from the foundation, a great sandpile was growing,
a neighbor with a wagon and a team of mules having
already brought in several loads of riverbed sand.
Everyone knew that Ned had some use for it, but he
had not yet divulged to them just what use that was.
In the meantime, children played in the huge sandpile. As the men were about to finish their coffee
and were thinking about going to work, someone
shouted from off to the west. The words were Cherokee.

"Dagwalela dagaluhga."

A wagon was coming. Several men jumped up
and ran toward the voice. A few of them carried
guns, just in case. Ned sat still and sipped at his
coffee. In a few moments, one of the men came
walking back.

"It's Old Wolf's boy," he said.

"Driving a wagon?" asked Arch Christie.

"Yeah," said the other. "Well, I don't know for sure who's driving it. That mule might be driving it, but Young Archie's riding on the seat."

"Another load of sand?" asked another man.

"It didn't look like a load of sand," said the other. "It looked like something else. I don't know what."

The wagon rolled into view in the distance, and most of the people left around the home site got up to go meet it.

"*Gadousdi na?*" someone asked. "What is that?"

When the wagon finally stopped, just by the place where the logs were stacked, Ned stood up. Young Wolf set the brake and tied the reins, and then he stood up in the wagon as if he were on a stage. He held his arms out to his sides, and everyone else stopped talking.

"It's a portable sawmill," he said. "*Asuhgwalosgi.* This is a Kenwood vertical steam engine, and this is a ball-bearing, combination nip, cutoff, and band-saw machine with a belt drive. They mount on one base, and the steam engine runs the saw. Now I need some strong backs to help me unload it and set it up."

Ned smiled.

"Where'd you get that?" someone asked.

"I don't think you want to know," said Young Wolf, "but it sure will make squaring off those logs a whole lot easier."

The portable sawmill was unloaded, and the vertical steam engine and the bad-bearing saw on its angle steel frame were bolted down to the same base and stabilized. The steam engine's firebox was stuffed with wood, and a fire was started. Water was poured into its boiler. Soon the engine was chuffing and the saw was whirring. The first log was run through four times, and it was squared. The men divided themselves up into small work units. One group started a second log on the saw, while a second group started to work notching the already squared log. Another group would stack and fit the logs, actually building the walls. Young Archie Wolf tended the steam engine, keeping its fire hot, keeping enough water in the boiler, checking its pressure valve. Ned was pleased. His house would be done in record time with all these good friends and with this new sawmill. Sure enough, the walls were up in a few days, and they were chinked with clay. They were high walls. This house, like the other one, would have a loft.

"Are we ready to start on the roof?" asked one of the men.

"Not yet," said Ned. "Next we build four more walls, right around these."

"A double-walled cabin?" said Young Wolf.

"That's right," said Ned.

It was two cabins, all right, one build right around the other. They left a space of about a foot between the walls. When all the walls were finally up, and all the spaces chinked, then they learned Ned's purpose for the sand. It was poured between the walls in the one-foot space that had been left there. When the space was filled, the roof was constructed. With the portable sawmill, they not only could square logs, they could also rip logs into boards. The inte-

rior walls of the new house were finished with up-
right one-by-six planks. A solid door was built, and
solid window covering panels which could be closed
and securely latched from the inside. Upstairs, in the
loft, narrow slits were cut. That made it difficult for
anyone outside to shoot at someone on the inside,
but someone inside could fire easily through the slits.
Finished, it was a larger, more comfortable house
than their last one. It was also nearly impregnable.
Young Archie Wolf stood back and looked at the
house the day they finished.

"I thought we were building a house," he said.
"This is a fort."

And they named it that day after what Young
Wolf had said. They called it Ned Christie's Fort.

There was still work to be done, but Ned and his
family no longer had to live in the cave. There was
furniture to be built, a table and chairs, beds, shelves,
and there was a new shop needed so that Ned's business could be resumed. And the workers returned
day after day. The shop walls went up, and the basic
furniture was made. At last Ned called a halt to the
gadugi, the cooperative labor group formed to help
a neighbor in need.

"You've all done enough," he said. "Thank you.
Wado."

"We'll still keep watch for the lawmen," said
Young Wolf. "If they come back, they won't surprise you again."

Ned raised his voice a little, just enough to make
sure that everyone could hear.

"I want you all to come back in four days," he said. "We'll kill a hog, and we'll have a big feast with all our friends to celebrate this new house. Come back in four days."

That evening, Old Wolf came to Ned Christie's Fort. He was carrying with him his bag of medicines, and he gave Ned some tobacco and told him where and when to smoke it. Then Old Wolf went back outside. He took his pipe, and some tobacco, and a match out of the bag, put the bag down by the door, and walked toward the east, seven steps away from the house. He stood facing the east, and he filled his pipe and lit it. He stood there for a while smoking, and then, from inside the house, they could hear his soft voice. He might have been singing. The voice stopped, and he smoked again as he walked around the house making a large circle. He stopped a quarter of the way around and stood facing north. There he smoked for a moment, and there he sang again, if it was singing. He walked again and smoked again, another quarter of the circle. He stopped to face the west. He smoked. He sang maybe. He walked, smoking, to the south, and he stopped there. He smoked a while longer, and then his soft voice once more floated out into the air, and it had the sound of smoke, and the smoke from his pipe had the look of a song. Then he walked back to the east, to the spot where he had started, and the circle around the house was closed. He stood there and puffed a few more times on the pipe until it went out. He walked back up to the front door where he had left his bag, and he reached in for something, a smaller bag. He drew that out and walked back to the spot where he had begun the circle, where he had finished the circle, the spot facing east. He stuck his wrinkled old brown fist into the bag and brought out a handful of something. It might have been crushed tobacco. It might have been something else. It had a dusty look about it though. He started to walk the big, counterclockwise circle again, this time sprinkling the dusty substance along behind himself as he went. At each of the four directional points, he stuffed his hand back into the bag for another handful. He did this until he had again closed the circle back at the place he had started, back at the spot facing the east. Then he was done.

That night in the new house, they burned cedar, and they smoked. Ned and Gatey and Arch all smoked. They smoked the tobacco Old Wolf had given them. They smoked it at the doors. (The new house, Ned Christie's Fort, had a back door. They would not again be trapped inside like rats.) They smoked the tobacco at each of the windows. They smoked it in each corner of the house and up in the loft and there by the slits that were cut for shooting at someone outside. The smoke filled the house, and it touched everything, every board, each piece of furniture, every inch of the walls and floor and ceiling. It crept into every nook and cranny and crack as only smoke can do, and then they slept. And that night in the new house, they slept well. They were all well protected. They were protected by the double walls and the packed sand, by the heavy doors and the window panels with their strong, inside latches. They were protected by the dogs outside who would warn them if anyone came close. They were protected by their neighbors, who also kept watch. They were protected by the two strong circles of Old Wolf's medicine. And inside the house, cleaned, oiled, loaded, and within easy reach, were Ned Christie's guns.

Chapter 11

Dave Rusk had readily agreed to lead a posse to Ned Christie's Fort. He had even been just a little afraid that he might have appeared to be too eager, but Yoes had given him the assignment and the authority to pick his own men. Rusk wanted to be the man to get Ned Christie. The famous Heck Thomas had failed, and Rusk was secretly more than a little jealous of Heck Thomas's reputation. Rusk had been a captain of cavalry in the Army of the Confederacy during the Civil War, and he had been a deputy United States marshal since 1875. He had more experience than Heck Thomas had. He knew that he was a better shot than Thomas was. For a while he had earned his living as a trick shot performer with a circus. And it hadn't been fake either. No shotgun loads in pistol bullets the way some of them did. On top of all that, Rusk thought that he knew the Cherokee Nation and the Cherokees. He had his business in the Cherokee Nation, the store there at Oaks, and

nearly all his customers were Cherokees. He even
had a Cherokee employee, a full blood, a young man
named Billy Israel. He had his home there at Oaks,
and he and his family got along well with their Cherokee neighbors. Of course, they did most of their
socializing with the nearly white mixed-bloods and
with the teachers and missionaries there at the Oaks
Mission School.

But Dave Rusk knew that he was the right man
for the job. At first he had resented the fact that Heck
Thomas had been selected over him to go after Ned
Christie. But now that Thomas had failed, he realized that it was better this way. It would make Rusk
look much better when he succeeded where Thomas
had failed. And it was a tougher job than it had been
when Thomas had tried it, for now Ned Christie was
expecting to be attacked. Thomas had surprised him.
And word had trickled out somehow that Ned Christie had built a fortress, and that he was being surrounded by loyal followers. Getting Ned Christie
now, after all this had happened, would propel
Rusk's own reputation as a top-notch lawman way
out in front of Thomas's. And that was what Dave
Rusk wanted. And so he had accepted the assignment, and he had made his plans. Eight men should
be enough, he decided, and they should all be Cherokees, all except Rusk himself, of course. He would
not approach any full-bloods for this job, for they
were nearly all in sympathy with the outlaw, but
many of the mixed-bloods were not. Still, he would
ease into conversation with them. One never knew
what to expect from a Cherokee.

The front door of the store opened, and Billy Israel
looked up from behind the counter to see two men
step in. The heavier of the two men was maybe five
feet eight inches tall, and he might have weighed
one-hundred-and-eighty pounds. He had blond,
wavy hair and steely blue eyes. The other man was
an inch or two shorter and twenty or thirty pounds
lighter. He looked younger than the bigger man, and
his hair was darker. Other than that, they looked
alike.

"Can I help you?" said Israel.

"I'm Monte Miller," said the older one. "This is
my brother Dean. We're supposed to meet Dave
Rusk here."

"Mr. Rusk is in the back room," said Israel. "The
others are all here, I think."

Dean Miller looked at his brother. "What others?"
he said.

The older Miller shrugged. "Hell," he said, "I
don't know."

Israel went to a door in the back wall and held it
open for the Miller brothers. They walked across the
room and through the door.

"Thanks," said the younger Miller. Israel closed
the door behind them. There was a long table in the
room. Dave Rusk sat at the head of the table, and
there were five other men sitting along its sides.
Rusk stood up when the Millers came into the room.

"Howdy, boys," he said. "Come on in and grab a
chair."

The Millers sat at the two remaining empty chairs, and Rusk sat down again.

"Well," he said, "we're all here. I don't know if y'all know each other or not. Down there is Monte Miller and his brother Dean. Next is Charlie Holtz, Stanley Bragg, Bood Whitmire, Hargis Hampton, and right here is Silas McMinn."

The seven men glanced around the table at each other.

"I've talked to each one of you individually," Rusk went on, "but I never let on to you just exactly what I wanted. That's why I've asked you all to come here together like this, so I can tell you all at once. I've been authorized by Fort Smith to put together a posse to go after Ned Christie."

Rusk paused for effect, and he looked around the table at each man there. None of the hard cases gave any indication of reaction to his opening remarks.

"You men are my choice," he went on. "You're all good men. I know that about you, and that's one of the reasons I picked you. But the other reason is this. This Ned Christie case is a hot potato. It's political as hell here in the Cherokee Nation. I guess you all know that. Most of the full-bloods seem to take his side. But I think that it's important that Ned Christie be taken by Cherokees. For one thing, you know the territory and you know the Cherokee habits better than anyone from the outside. The other thing is that it will not look as much like a political thing if he's caught by Cherokees. Do y'all understand my point?"

The seven men nodded their heads affirmatively.

"All right," said Rusk. "Now, I think I know how you men all feel about this deal, but just to be sure, I think we ought to talk over a few things before this goes any farther. First thing I need to know is this: How do you all feel about Ned Christie?"

Rusk looked at Monte Miller when he asked the question. Miller sat slumped in his chair.

"I don't know the man," he said. "He's wanted by the law, I guess. That's all I know."

"But what have you heard about the case?" said Rusk.

"Nothing," said Miller.

Rusk's eyes moved on down the line to Dean Miller. The younger Miller jerked a thumb toward his brother.

"What he said," said Dean Miller.

Rusk looked toward Charlie Holtz. "Charlie?" he said.

"The man's a killer," said Holtz. "He killed a United States lawman."

"Any doubt in your mind about that?" asked Rusk.

"Why should there be?" said Holtz. "I got no reason to disbelieve the charges that's been made."

"Is there anyone here with a different opinion on that question?" said Rusk, looking over the faces at the table. No one responded. Finally Bood Whitmire broke the silence.

"I reckon not," he said.

"Then my next question is this," said Rusk. "Ned Christie's a dangerous man. He killed Dan Maples, and he shot Larry Isbel in the shoulder, crippling

him up real bad. He fought off Heck Thomas and
five more men. Heck Thomas is supposed to be the
best in the business. They say Ned Christie's a crack
shot, and they say that now he has built himself a
log fort. They also say he's got a gang around him
now."

"I didn't get the question," said Monte Miller.

"The question is this," said Rusk. "Do you have
any qualms about going after the man I have just
described?"

"Does that mean are we scared of him?" said
Whitmire.

"Well, yeah," said Rusk. "That's part of what it
means."

"I ain't met the man I'm scared of," said Whitmire.

"Anyone?" said Rusk. "Any qualms?"

Some shook their heads, some shruggad. No one
offered any verbal response to the question.

"All right then," said Rusk. "I have one more
question. How do you feel about the politics involved?"

"How's politics got anything to do with going after a killer?" said the older Miller brother.

"Can any of you all answer that question for Mr.
Miller?" said Rusk. "After all, it's Cherokee politics,
and I'm not a Cherokee. I'm just a resident here."

"Ned Christie belongs to the Nighthawks," said
Hargis Hampton. "That's a full-blood group. They
wouldn't let any of us join them if we wanted to.
The way I understand it, the Nighthawks wants to
move backwards. They want to keep everything In-

dian. They want to keep talking Cherokee. They want to practice the old heathen religion. They tried to keep the railroad out of the Cherokee Nation. Right now, their big thing is holding off the Dawes Act. You know, the allotment business. The government wants to give us all our own land. The Nighthawks don't believe in that. They want the land to stay like it is, to be all owned by the Cherokee Nation. Is that what you're getting at, Dave?"

"Yeah," said Rusk. "I think so. Ned Christie has come to represent that radical political point of view to a great many Cherokees. At least it seems that way to me. And before we ride out there after him, and before the bullets start to fly, I want to know where you all stand on that point."

"It seems to me," said McMinn, "that we all stand to profit from this allotment business."

"If they give us land," said the older Miller, "could we sell it?"

"Hell, yes," said Holtz. "If it's my own land, your damn rights I could sell it, if I was of a mind to."

"Is anyone here in sympathy with the Nighthawk point of view on this matter?" said Rusk.

Again there was a pause, and again, Bood Whitmire broke the silence.

"I reckon not," he said.

"Well," said Rusk, "I was pretty sure what your answers would be or I wouldn't have asked you here, but I just thought that we ought to get all that out in the open before we went any farther on this deal."

"I have a question," said the older Miller.

"What is it, Monte?" said Rusk.

"How much do we get paid?"

That same day a large crowd was gathered around
Ned Christie's Fort. All the people who had helped
to build the Fort and the new shop, all the people
who had helped Ned and Gatey and Arch through
their recent trouble when Ned and Arch had been
wounded and when the Christie family had been living in the cave, all their friends and neighbors and
relatives were gathered there. And a great feast was
spread out before them. There was plenty for everyone to eat: fresh hog meat, corn bread, bean bread,
wild greens and eggs, corn, green beans, brown
beans, tripe soup, dried corn soup. And there were
pots and pots of coffee.

As usual the old men were seated and served first,
and among them was a special guest. Old Watt
Christie, Ned's father, had come from his own home
several miles away. Everyone ate his fill, and then
some, and then the men strolled down to the marble
yard. Ned missed his first toss. It was the first time
he had played since the big fight, the first time for
him to toss a marble with only his left eye. Well, he
thought, it would take a few times. He had practiced
shooting since losing the right eye, and he was
shooting well again. A little practice here and the
marble tossing would be as good as ever. It would
be good for him, too, this practice. He had to learn
to compensate totally for the lost eye. The others got
ahead of him, but on his third toss, he hit his target,
and the sound of his marble striking the other was

almost like the sound of a gunshot. He had it. They played the game until it was too dark for them to see the holes at which they were throwing or the marbles on the ground, and Ned Christie had won the game.

They walked back up the hillside to the house, and Ned sat across the table from Old Watt. They talked about the weather. They talked about the crops. They even talked politics some, but they did not talk about the lawmen and the purpose of the fort. Ned invited his father to spend the night in the Fort, and Arch Christie extended the same invitation to Young Archie Wolf. Everyone else eventually went home.

The following morning in front of the store in Oaks, Dave Rusk met his seven deputies. They were all well mounted and heavily armed. Rusk made sure that they all had plenty of ammunition. He expected to be successful, but he also anticipated a good fight. The ride to Ned Christie's Fort would take the best part of the day, and Rusk wanted to get an early start. He figured that they could get near the Fort by late evening, and then stop for a rest. He was not yet sure whether they would attack that night or wait until the following morning. It would depend on how long the trip would take them and how tired the men and horses were at the end of the ride. He would wait to make that decision at the end of the trail. One way or another, he would be meeting Ned Christie soon. He assumed that there would be either bodies or wounded men on the return trip, so he had a wagon and team ready, and he had Bood Whitmire leave his saddle horse behind with Billy Israel and drive the wagon. The wagon also contained food, blankets, and extra ammunition.

Chapter 12

The posse made good time. They found a likely camping spot within a couple of miles of Ned Christie's Fort, and they stopped to rest and to eat. Rusk had still not made up his mind about when they would attack. He noticed, though, that the members of his posse couldn't seem to sit still. They kept moving about the campsite, talking to each other, looking off into the woods in the direction of Ned Christie's Fort. There was still plenty of daylight, lots of time to kill a man. Rusk made his decision, but he kept it to himself.

Ned Christie was outside when Youngbird came running toward him, waving a hand. The two Archies had gone into the house to see if Gatey would give them something to eat. Old Watt had already left to go back home.

"Ned. Ned," called Youngbird. He was almost out of breath from running.

"What is it?" said Ned.

Youngbird panted and pointed toward the west.

"Eight men," he said. "They're camped about two miles west. Seven of them riding horseback. One driving a wagon. They've all got guns."

Ned put a hand on Youngbird's shoulder.

"Thank you, friend," he said.

"It looks like a posse," said Youngbird.

"Yes," said Ned. "It probably is a posse. I'll be ready for them. They might wait until morning, but they could come yet tonight. I'll get ready now. You go on before they get here."

"I can stay and help you," said Youngbird.

"No," said Ned. "You've already done your part. You've helped already. We'll be all right. Go on now."

Rusk decided that both men and horses had rested long enough. There was no reason to wait until morning. He was anxious, and he could tell that the other seven men were almost as anxious as he was.

"Let's go in," he said.

"What about the wagon?" said Whitmire.

"Bring up the rear," said Rusk. "I'll tell you when to stop it. All right, let's get saddled up. Toss all the gear in the wagon."

The camp was broken in a matter of minutes, and all the camping gear was loaded into the wagon. The horses were saddled, and the men, except Whitmire, climbed into their saddles. Whitmire was on the wagon seat.

"Come on," said Rusk, and he spurred his horse

and headed for Ned Christie's Fort at a gallop. The others fell in behind him, and last of all Whitmire clattered along in the wagon.

Ned Christie went inside the house.

"We've got company coming," he said, and he looked at his son. "Bring in some fresh water. We might be inside for a while."

"I'll help you," said Archie Wolf, and the two Archies went outside. Ned took his Winchester up into the loft along with two extra boxes of shells. Then he went back down and strapped one of his Colts on around his waist. He had only the one holster. He stuck the other Colt in his waistband, got some extra bullets for the Colts, and went back up into the loft. The door opened down below, and the two Archies came in rolling the water barrel. They set it just beside the door.

"Go on home now, Archie," said Ned. "There's still time."

"I'll stay," said Young Archie. "I've got my rifle."

Ned started to say something else, then changed his mind.

"Shut the door and bolt it," he said. "Check the back door and all the windows, too."

He looked out the slit. No one was coming yet, as far as he could see. And the dogs were quiet. Maybe the men Youngbird had seen weren't coming after him at all. Then he saw them, and then the dogs began to bark.

———

Rusk put up his right hand to call a halt, and he hauled back on the reins of his horse at the same time.

"Dismount," he shouted. "Bood, stay with the horses and the wagon. The rest of you, come on."

Following the lead of Rusk, the six deputies ran into the woods just enough to make use of the cover. Then they started toward the Fort. If they continued uninterrupted, they would move along the tree line behind the Fort. But they didn't get that far. Ned Christie was watching, and as soon as Rusk was near enough, Ned fired. He shot ahead of Rusk on purpose. It was a warning shot, Ned's way of telling them that they could still turn around and get out. Rusk ducked behind a tree. Then he raised his own rifle and sent a shot at the Fort. The six deputies behind him started firing too.

"Hold it," shouted Rusk. "Hold it."

The firing stopped.

"Move on up here," he called. "Be careful."

The six men made their ways through the edge of the woods to join Rusk. He moved back a short ways into the woods for safety.

"We're getting nowhere like that," he said. "Look. He's up there in the loft. See that slit up there? That's what he's shooting out of."

"So what do we do?" said Hampton.

"All right. Look," said Rusk. "I want four of you back up there at the edge of the trees. Just about where I was at. Keep him occupied there. I want Charlie to work his way on around behind the house. I'm going to make a try for the shop building there.

We'll be on three sides that way. Stan, when Charlie's in place, you sneak on over and join him. Okay?"

"Yeah," said Stanley Bragg.

"And when I get in place, Hargis, you come and join me. That will leave the Miller brothers and Silas here. All right, get up there and start shooting. As soon as they start, Charlie, you and me will take off."

The Millers, Bragg, Hampton, and McMinn moved to the edge of the woods and began shooting at the slit in the logs. Rusk ran for the shop, and Charlie Holtz started through the woods toward the back of the house. In a moment, Stanley Bragg elbowed Hargis Hampton. Hampton lowered his rifle and looked at Bragg.

"Now?" said Bragg.

"Yeah," said Hampton. "Let's go."

Hampton ran toward the shop as Bragg started after Holtz behind the house. The others kept shooting.

Inside the house, up in the loft, Ned Christie sat with his back to the wall just beside the slit in the logs. The bullets that found their way through the small opening went into the ceiling or into the walls high up. Most of the bullets were not even getting into the house. Arch Christie's head appeared over the edge of the loft. He was coming up the ladder.

"Keep down," said Ned.

Arch crawled on up onto the loft, but once up

there, he bellied along to where Ned sat. Behind him came Archie Wolf with his rifle.

"You could use some help," said Young Wolf.

Ned pulled the Colt revolver out of the waistband of his trousers and handed it to his son. He pointed toward another gun port on the back wall, and Arch crawled over to it. Young Wolf gave Ned a questioning look, and Ned motioned for him to move to the wall opposite Ned's post. There, too, was a gun port, another vertical slit in the logs. Archie Wolf moved over to that one. The rifles of the posse continued to roar outside, and bullets continued to thud into the outside wall of the Fort. Now and then a shot made it inside. Arch Christie pressed himself against the wall the way his father had done, but knowing that the shots from outside were all being aimed at the other wall, he decided to sneak a look outside. He peeked through the port in the back wall just in time to see Bragg move from one tree to another. He eased the big Colt up into position and waited. Bragg moved again, and Arch fired.

"Ah. God damn."

Bragg dropped to the ground with a bullet in his right thigh. He managed to hang on to his rifle with his right hand, but he reached over with his left to clutch at the wound. Blood gushed between his fingers.

"I'm hit," he said. "Charlie. Charlie, where are you? I'm hit."

Arch Christie watched as Charlie Holtz came out from behind his cover to assist the wounded Bragg. He looked over at Ned.

"I hit one," he said. "There's another one back here trying to help him."

"Let them go," said Ned. "Just keep watching."

Outside, Holtz helped Bragg to his feet. With an arm around Holtz's shoulder and his rifle serving as a cane, Bragg managed to hobble. The two deputies retreated through the woods, heading for the wagon. It would be a long and painful walk for Bragg.

Rusk and Hampton had worked their way around to the front of the shop. Rusk was in the lead. He pressed his back against the wall and sneaked a look around the corner. He could see the gun port the deputies were shooting at from the woods. He moved back again.

"Hargis," he said. "I can see that slit from here. I'll fire into it. You run for the front door."

"Okay," said Hampton.

Rusk raised his rifle and fired, and Hampton started to run. Just then the barrel of Ned Christie's Winchester was poked out the port. Ned fired, and Hampton spun backward and to his left, hit in the left shoulder. He dropped his own rifle as he landed on his face. Rusk fired again at the port.

"Get back here," he shouted.

Hampton crawled in the dirt leaving a trail of blood until he was back behind the wall of the shop with Rusk. He struggled up to his knees, turned and sat down on the ground, leaning back against the shop wall. Rusk squatted down beside him to look at the wound.

"Damn," said Hampton. "I'm bleeding like a stuck pig."

"Come on," said Rusk. "I've got to get you out of here."

He helped Hampton to his feet, and they walked back around the shop. They would have to make a run for the cover of the woods. They could head straight back for the wagon in comparative safety, but Rusk didn't want to go back to the wagon.

"Can you make it on your own?" he said.

"I don't know," said Hampton. "I'm feeling kind of weak. I'll try,"

Rusk waved his arm, trying to get the attention of Whitmire back at the wagon, but it didn't work. He couldn't tell what Whitmire was doing.

"Well," he said to Hampton, "go ahead. Get started. I'll send someone after you to help. Go on."

Hampton started walking toward the wagon. Rusk watched him for a moment, then turned and made a dash for the woods. Soon he had rejoined the other deputies. They stopped firing when Rusk appeared.

"Hargis is hit," Rusk said. "Silas, catch up with him and help him back to the wagon."

"All right," said McMinn. "But Stanley's hit too. Charlie took him back."

"God damn," said Rusk. "Well, go on, but when you get him there, come on back. No. Wait a minute. You stay there with them. Send Bood back."

"Okay," said McMinn, and he started on his way. For about half the distance to the wagon, McMinn was covered by the shop, but the rest of the way he was vulnerable. But it would take a good long shot, an extremely good shot, to bring a man down at that distance.

From his gun port, Ned Christie saw McMinn running toward the wagon. He took careful aim and slowly squeezed the trigger, and he watched as McMinn stumbled and fell forward. Up ahead of McMinn, Hampton was slowly making his way back. He was walking like a drunk, staggering and weaving. He did not even look back to see McMinn fall, but from the wagon, Bood Whitmire saw. There were now two wounded men out there, one staggering toward the wagon, the other writhing on the ground. Stanley Bragg was already in the wagon, having been brought back by Charlie Holtz. Whitmire thought for only an instant, then he ran toward the wounded men. He reached Hampton first, and he paused.

"Hargis," he said, "keep going. Silas is back there. He's down. I got to go to him first."

Hampton did not respond, but he did keep moving, however unsteadily. Whitmire ran on toward McMinn, but he didn't make it. A second shot from the gun port broke his knee.

Rusk and the two Miller brothers saw what happened.

"Dave," said the older Miller. "Dave, half of us is hurt."

"We better get out of here," said the younger Miller. "Don't you think? Huh?"

Rusk looked toward the wagon and thought of the four wounded men. He shot another glance toward the Fort and thought about Ned Christie. He thought about Heck Thomas and his reputation as a gunfighting lawman.

"Damn," he said. "Let's go."

Rusk and the Millers stayed in the woods for as long as they could.

"All right," said Rusk. "Let's help those boys over to the wagon, but be careful. Keep an eye on that damn Fort."

There were still two wounded men out in the open. Hampton had finally reached the wagon on his own. Rusk held his rifle ready and looked toward Ned Christie's gun port.

"Monte, Dean," he said, "go get those boys and bring them in. I'll keep you covered."

From his loft Ned had a clear shot at the Millers. He thought that he could probably even hit the one standing back there with the rifle in his hands, but four of the lawmen were wounded, and the others were pulling out. They were obviously loading up the wounded to leave. There was no need to shoot anymore.

"It's all right, boys," he said to the two Archies. "They're leaving."

The Millers helped the two wounded deputies back to the wagon, and with all four of the injured men in the wagon, Monte Miller climbed onto the wagon seat to drive. The other healthy lawmen climbed into their saddles, and the retreat began. Rusk was the last one to ride out, and just before he did, he turned for one last look at Ned Christie's Fort. He raised the rifle in his right hand over his head in a defiant gesture, and he shouted back toward the Fort.

"Ned Christie, you son of a bitch," he said. "I'll be back."

Chapter 13

After the battle, after the shooting and the shouts, after the clattering of horses' hooves and the rattling of the wagon, the calm was almost oppressive. The defenders of the stronghold unlatched the doors and windows and let fresh air into the house, and they went outside. The enemy had been routed. The lawmen were all gone. The dogs ran around anxiously, sniffing at the places the deputies had been, licking at the spots of blood they found here and there. Gradually the birds came back and started to sing again. Squirrels chattered and scolded. Ned stood outside and looked at his log house, at Ned Christie's Fort. There was no visible evidence of the attack. His wife walked over to stand beside him, and he put an arm around her shoulders.

"Is this the way it will be," she said, "from now on?"

"Yes," he said. "They won't stop now, and they won't listen to me."

"But you didn't kill that man," she protested.

"No," he said, "but now I've shot five of Judge Parker's darlings."

"Yes," she said.

They would not talk about it again. It was just something that had been added to their way of life. Every day's business would include being ready for an attack, watching, listening, staying constantly prepared. Ned could drive them off, but they would return, again and again, until it was finally over.

And they did come back. Two months later Rusk brought another posse. This time there were ten, and they attacked from the woods across the valley clearing. Ned shot two of them, and they left. But he recognized Rusk, though he did not know the man's name, from the previous attack. Six weeks later they came again. Ten men again. Again the same leader. Ned shot one in the hip. He shot another in the arm. Then, while Rusk was peering around the edge of a tree, he took careful aim and shot the hat off the deputy's head. Rusk, white with fear and trembling, called a retreat.

Youngbird found Ned Christie out in the yard salvaging usable parts off an old wagon.

" 'Siyo, Nede, " he said.

" 'Siyo, " said Ned, returning the greeting. He laid aside his hammer. "You want some coffee?"

"Sure," said Youngbird. He waited outside while Ned went into the house. In a couple of minutes, Ned returned with two cups of coffee, and he and

Youngbird sat down in front of the shop on two homemade stools. They sipped their coffee and made small talk for a few minutes, before Youngbird decided to let Ned know why he had come.

"That man who's been coming here," he said, "the one who has been leading the posses, his name is Dave Rusk. He's a white man, but he lives at Oaks. The store there belongs to him."

He paused to sip his coffee. Ned said nothing, so Youngbird continued.

"The men he brings with him are all white Cherokees. Mixed-bloods. They say that he thinks Cherokees should get you. Politics. There's a Cherokee boy who works for Rusk in his store. He's a real Cherokee."

Ned's eyes narrowed to dark slits as he quietly sipped hot coffee from his cup.

"They say that Rusk wants to get you real bad," said Youngbird. "They say that other one, that Heck Thomas, he was a famous lawman, and he couldn't do it. So Rusk thinks that if he does it after Heck Thomas failed, that will make him a famous lawman."

Ned Christie stood up and paced away from Youngbird. He stood for a moment staring off across the valley clearing toward the woods on the other side.

"Dave Rusk, you said?"

"Yes," said Youngbird. "That's his name."

"This Dave Rusk, this white man who is a guest in the Cherokee Nation, wants to kill me, or at least arrest me and take me to Fort Smith to hang," said

Ned. "And he wants to do that in order to make himself famous."

"That's what they say about him up around Oaks," said Youngbird.

"And he's using Cherokees against me?"

"Yes. Those breeds."

"Have you been to Oaks?" said Ned.

"Yes. I went up there for a few days."

"Did you see the store that this man owns?"

"I even went inside and bought a can of peaches. I bought them from *Wili*. Billy Israel. That's his name in English. He's a full-blood Cherokee. He even talked in Cherokee to me when I bought the peaches."

"My friend," said Ned, "up until now, I've done nothing except stay home and defend myself. I think that I will go to Oaks."

"I'll go with you," said Youngbird.

Ned looked at Youngbird. He had never asked anyone to get involved in his problems. It was enough that he had been made an outlaw. He didn't want to be responsible for making anyone else play that role. But he hadn't asked Youngbird. Youngbird had volunteered. And this was the second time he had done so. The first time Ned had told him to go on home and stay out of it. He gave Youngbird an affirmative nod of the head.

"When will we go?" asked Youngbird.

"Tonight," said Ned. "We'll ride at night and be there in the morning when the store opens up for business."

———

At about the same time in Oaks, Dave Rusk was loading all of his family's belongings from the small house where they lived into a wagon.

"I don't see why we have to rush out of here so quickly," Mrs. Rusk was saying.

"Look," said Rusk. "Ned Christie's a dangerous man. He's a vicious man. I don't want my family to be in any danger. He knows where I live. The word has come to me that he knows I'm the one who's been trying to get him. I don't want anything to happen to you or the kids just because Ned Christie's after me. We're moving over to Joplin and that's that."

"But so quickly," said Mrs. Rusk.

"The sooner the better," said Rusk. "I want you all to be safe."

Ned Christie sat alone. He thought about the Dave Rusk posses. He thought about the Cherokee mixed-bloods, the Cherokees who looked like white men, the Cherokees who acted like white men and thought like white men. And he thought about white men like Dave Rusk, white men who lived in the Cherokee Nation. The population of the Cherokee Nation was beginning to look more white than Indian. He wondered about the future of the Cherokee Nation. What did it hold? What surprises? What miseries? What would the Cherokee Nation look like in another ten years? Would there be a Cherokee Nation in another ten years? Ten short years. Would there be Cherokees? Of course, he thought, there would always be Cherokees. But will the Cherokees have their own home? He began to think that it was a hopeless battle he was waging, a fight that he could not win. Yet he would not stop. He would not surrender. He would not hang at Fort Smith as a common criminal, as a murderer, for a crime he did not commit. He would fight back for as long as he could fight.

But thinking about the future, he was sad. He was sad for his son. He was sad for all the young people, and for the Cherokees yet unborn. Their future did not appear to be very bright. The Cherokees were walking a long, dark path, a path which pointed ever west, toward the land where the Sun lived, toward the place they knew as the Darkening Land, which was inhabited by the souls of the dead.

Once again his thoughts focused on Rusk and on what he was planning to do about the man, and he realized that this war he was waging, this futile, one-man war with the United States deputy marshals, was personal on one level, yes, but it was much more than that. It had to do with what was right and what was wrong. It had to do with things like jurisdiction and sovereignty, and it had to do with the schemes of the United States government regarding the future of the Cherokee Nation. It was all about *duyukduh*, the Truth, the great spiritual laws of the universe, the immutable and irrefutable laws of God and man and decent behavior. Rusk was at the same time symbolic of all these things that were wrong, of the overweening arrogance of those who, because of greed or excessive pride, would lash out at the Earth itself or at the Sun, and he was an individual. He was a man. He was a white man who was living in the Cherokee Nation, and he was abusing that sacred privilege. He was using Cherokee people against Cherokee people. To Ned's mind, that was appalling. What he had in mind for Rusk would be revenge, yes, but it would also be justice. For once justice would be served, even if Ned Christie had to administer that justice himself.

He sat outside alone. He had said goodbye to his wife. He was waiting. His horse was saddled. His guns were loaded. There was extra ammunition in the saddlebags. The rifle was sheathed there on the left side of the saddle. One of his Colt revolvers was in the holster there at his right side and the other was tucked into his belt. Then he heard the sounds of approaching horses and a rolling wagon. He was not startled or surprised by this. He had been waiting for those sounds. He stood up and walked to his horse and swung himself up into the saddle. Arch Christie rode up first. Behind him was the wagon, driven by young Archie Wolf. Then came Youngbird and Sanders and Johnny Spade. All were well mounted and well armed.

"Why the wagon?" someone had said earlier.

Ned's answer had been short.

"We're going shopping," he had said.

Chapter 14

They were waiting right there when he opened. The sun was barely up. Pinks and reds and yellows danced across the tops of the tree-covered hills that formed the distant horizon. Birds sang and squirrels chattered, and people, too, were beginning to stir in the tiny community of Oaks, a community that had grown up around a Lutheran mission. There wasn't much to it: the mission itself, a few scattered houses, Dave Rusk's store. Billy Israel nodded and spoke a Cherokee greeting as he opened the door and stepped inside. None of the six Cherokees lounging against the front wall of the store responded to his greeting. They waited until he had been inside for a few minutes. Then Ned Christie stood up. He nodded his head toward the door, and the other five Indians moved to follow him inside. Billy Israel noticed two things right away: The six men were all armed, and they looked surly. He was nervous.

"How can I help you?" he asked, still speaking Cherokee.

"Where's the white man who owns this store?" asked Ned.

"He's not here," said Israel, "but I work for him. Can I help you?"

"Where is he?" said Youngbird, taking a step toward Israel.

"He's on a trip."

Youngbird stepped in even closer to Israel.

"Does he live here at Oaks?" he asked.

"He did," said Israel, "but he's moving. He loaded up a wagon yesterday and left with his family."

Ned Christie was browsing, looking at various goods on the shelves. He picked up a large can of peaches.

"Do you like peaches?" he asked his son.

"Yes," said Arch. "I like peaches."

"We'll take some," said Ned, and he tossed the can to Arch. "Take some more. Put them in the wagon. Take all of them."

The two Archies began taking all the peaches off the shelf. Israel tried to count the cans, and he nervously scrawled a note, but all of a sudden, there were five men carrying goods outside and loading them into the wagon which stood waiting there in front of the store. Youngbird hauled out several bolts of calico. Sanders found a new pair of high-topped black leather boots which fit his feet. He tossed his old shoes on the floor, pulled on the new boots, and then began gathering up boxes of ammunition for all the guns. Spade was getting Polo Soap and Durham

and Union Leader tobacco. The Archies, having carried out all the peaches, were cleaning the Mocha &
Java and the Blanke's Mojav Coffee off the shelves.
Ned Christie alone was not shopping. He had walked
over to the counter and leaned an elbow on it. He
looked Israel in the eyes, a threatening gesture
among Cherokees.

"What is your white man's name?" he asked.

"Dave Rusk," said Israel. He looked down, trying
to avoid Ned's gaze, but his eyes kept darting back
up to the other man's, and the other's eyes still
stared steadily at him. Israel began to squirm.

"Where is he taking his family to live?" said Ned.

"He's taking them to Missouri," said Israel. "To
Joplin, I think."

"Do you know why he is moving?"

"I don't—I think for safety."

"Is it so dangerous to live here in the Cherokee
Nation? Is Oaks such an unfriendly community?"

"He is a United States deputy marshal," said Israel. "I guess he's made some enemies. I think he's
afraid for the safety of his family."

"Who is it that this lawman is afraid of?"

Israel hesitated for a moment before answering
that question. He shifted his weight nervously. He
glanced at Ned's steady gaze, then looked away
again.

"I think maybe he's afraid of Ned Christie," he
said.

"Do you know Ned Christie?" asked Ned.

"No."

"Do you know who I am?"

"No."

"I'm Ned Christie."

"I—"

Ned stared at Israel for another long and silent moment.

"What did you want to say?" he asked.

"I only work here at the store," said Israel.

"You work for a white man who is a guest in our country," said Ned. "We allow this man to live in our country. We even allow him to operate a business here. He's making money off of us. And how does he repay our kindness and our hospitality? How does he?"

"I—I don't know."

"Like most white men, he's greedy," said Ned. "He never has enough. And he has no gratitude. If you give him a hog, he doesn't say thank you. He says give me another one. If you give him Georgia and North Carolina and Alabama and Tennessee, he waits only a little while, and then he says, now give me this Indian Territory. So this Rusk has his store in our country, and he makes money from our people, but he's not satisfied with that. He also works as a lawman for the United States, and he comes into our country to arrest or kill his hosts. For more money. Do you think that's right?"

"I—I don't think about that," said Israel.

"Maybe you should," said Ned. "Maybe you should."

Slowly, during the preceding conversation, the other five men had gathered around Ned, and Israel was beginning to wilt under their hard stares. Ned turned to face them.

"Have you finished your shopping?" he asked.

"The wagon's full," said Arch Christie. "We can't load anything else."

"Well," said Ned, "we can't leave things like this. *Akinaluh-ha*."

"Oh," said Youngbird, "he's getting angry now."

"Yes," said Ned, "and do you know what it is that's making me angry? It's not Dave Rusk and men like him. I expect that from white men. What makes me angry is the Cherokees who work for him. They join his posses and try to kill me. They work in his store to help make him rich with Cherokee money. That's what makes me angry."

With a sudden swipe of his arm, Ned cleared the counter top of boxes, cans, bottles, and papers. Taking the cue, Sanders kicked over the cracker barrel, and Spade pushed over an entire free-standing shelf unit. Before Arch Christie had time to make a move to join in the destructive melee, Ned caught his attention and nodded toward Israel.

"Get him out of here," he said.

The two Archies took Israel, each one holding him by an arm, and led the frightened, bewildered young man outside. Ned watched as Youngbird, Sanders, and Spade continued to overturn and smash everything in the store. Eventually Youngbird grew tired of the job and went outside. Spade and Sanders continued kicking, throwing, and stomping on things for a while, but finally, they, too, slowed down and stopped. They had nearly worn themselves out. They looked at Ned.

"Go on out," he said.

He stood alone and surveyed the mess he had caused to be made. Certainly this had hurt Rusk. He had been disappointed when he had learned that Rusk was not in Oaks, but maybe, he thought, this was better. Somehow it seemed to hurt a white man worse to lose his money than to lose even his life. Yes, maybe it was better this way after all. Rusk was not really important after all. Rusk was but one man. Even if Rusk had been in Oaks, even if Ned had killed Rusk, as he almost certainly would have done had he found the man, there would be more Rusks. There would always be more, more deputies, more posses, more white men in the Cherokee Nation, taking money, taking land, taking, always taking.

Ned kicked through the rubble on the floor until he found a box of Telegraph matches. He took one and struck it and watched as the match head exploded, fizzled, and finally settled down to a smooth-burning blue and yellow flame. Then he held the flame down under the pile of recently created debris and waited. The flame grew, and Ned dropped the match. It wouldn't take long. He walked to the door and turned back to watch a little longer. The flames began to crackle, and the fire began to spread. The match boxes which were under there caught and flared up, their initial burst dying down, and the fire looking smaller for an instant. But then it spread some more. Soon the whole place would be ablaze. Ned took a deep breath and expelled it in an audible

sigh. Then he stepped outside and shut the door behind himself. When he turned around he saw the
wagon, loaded almost to overflowing with the goods
from Rusk's store, and he saw the five saddle horses
waiting. He did not see the other five men, not immediately. He looked to his right, and there they
were. Not five but six men. For the other five still
had poor Billy Israel. They had a small fire going,
and on the fire was a pot of black tar. Sanders had
a stick in his hand, the end of which was dripping
with the black goo. Already some of it had been
daubed on poor Israel's back.

"Let him go," said Ned. "He's a Cherokee boy."

Joe Walker rushed toward the bench there in front
of the capitol building in Tahlequah. Peacheater and
Cabbagehead were sitting there, and Walker wanted
someone to talk to. He held in his hand a folded
newspaper as he hurried to the bench and sat down.

"See what I got here?" he said.

"It looks like a newspaper to me," said Peacheater. "What do you think?"

"It might be a newspaper," said Cabbagehead.

"Of course, it's a newspaper," said Walker. "It's
a recent one, too. It's in English, but I can read English. You want to know what it says?"

"I don't care what it says in that white man's
newspaper," said Cabbagehead. "It must be a bunch
of lies."

"If white man wrote it, it's a bunch of lies,"
agreed Peacheater.

"You don't know that," said Walker. "You can't even read English."

"White man never told us anything but lies," said Cabbagehead. "So that's all I need to know."

"There's a whole lot of stuff in this newspaper," said Walker. "There's even something in here about Victoria."

"Oh," said Peacheater, "I know Victoria. What does it say about her? Has she got herself a new husband? She left old Wally Bear last thing I heard."

"No," said Walker. "I mean Queen Victoria. See. If you could read English you'd know about these things. Don't you even know that Victoria is the queen of England?"

"I don't even know that there's such a place as England," said Cabbagehead. "Maybe that's another white man's lie. I never saw England."

"I think that maybe England's a real place," said Peacheater. "The white man had to come from somewhere. He sure didn't come from the same place we did. Maybe he came from that England."

"Or maybe he just fell out of the sky," said Cabbagehead. "Anyhow, I don't care about the queen of England. That Vicki."

"Victoria," said Walker. "You don't call the queen of England Vicki."

"I don't call her anything," said Peacheater, " 'cause I don't know her."

"I don't want to know her," said Cabbagehead. "Is she a white woman?"

"Of course she's white," said Walker. "She's an English lady."

"I don't want to know her," said Cabbagehead.

"Well," said Walker, opening up his paper, "that's not all that's in this paper. Look here. Here's a story about Ned Christie."

"What does that one say?" said Peacheater.

"Well," said Walker, reading and translating slowly, "it says that Ned Christie is still at large."

"I knew that," said Cabbagehead.

"It says that he's the worst outlaw ever in these parts."

Cabbagehead stood up, indignant, and took a couple of backwards steps so that he was facing Walker.

"How could that be?" he said. "The worst outlaw. Have those white men ever heard of Jesse James? Cole Younger? Who do they think they are anyhow? White man's newspaper."

Having got that out of his system, he sat back down.

"What else do they say about Ned Christie?" said Peacheater.

"They say he's got a fort up in the hills and a great big gang of outlaws in there with him. They say he's robbed a whole bunch of banks and trains and stagecoaches, and he's killed a whole bunch of men and raped a bunch of women. They say the Indian Territory won't be a safe place for decent folks to live in until Ned Christie is caught or killed."

Cabbagehead stood up again. This time he snatched the newspaper out of Walker's hands. He folded it back up and held it out in his right hand.

"You know what this white man's newspaper is

good for?" he asked Walker. "Well, I'll show you."

He took a wide stance and bent his knees. Then he reached between his legs with the newspaper and rubbed it along the seat of his britches in a more than slightly obscene gesture. Then he tossed it in Walker's lap.

"That's all it's good for," he said.

Walker stared for a moment at the newspaper in his lap. Then he stood up so that the paper fell to the ground.

"I don't want to touch it now," he said. "Not after what you did to it."

"Well, that's all it's good for," said Cabbagehead. "White man's newspaper. It's full of lies."

Peacheater chuckled as the wrinkled paper fluttered and rolled over in the breeze.

Chapter 15

Parker limped painfully up the front steps of the prison. He could hear the prisoners groaning, howling, and otherwise carrying on in the big cells down below. He tried to ignore the noise as well as the stench from down there. Pain shot through his hips as he climbed the stairs. He winced, and he groaned aloud. He stepped through the front door of the building, and he turned to his left to go into the marshal's office. Yoes came to his feet there behind his desk, a look of surprise on his face. It was not often that the judge made his painful way across the yard unless the court was in session. He usually sent for people to come to him. He opened his mouth as if to say something, but Parker spoke first.

"Look at this," he said, handing Yoes a piece of rumpled paper.

Yoes took the paper and read.

"It's from Washington," said Parker. "The eyes of Washington are on us here in Fort Smith. Ned Christie has got to be stopped. It's been four years, Mr. Yoes. Four long years. It's got to come to an end. Now. Everything we believe in, everything we stand for depends on this. Our reputations depend on this. Nothing else that we have accomplished, nothing that we may accomplish in the future will count for anything as long as Ned Christie is at large. People will not remember the number of criminals brought to justice. They will remember Ned Christie making fools of us. Mr. Yoes, my sleep is troubled by Ned Christie. I don't care what it costs, but I want it done. Drop everything else, if you have to, but get Ned Christie."

When Parker had finally left his office, Yoes sat down again. He rested his heavy head on his left hand while his right tapped nervously on his desktop. He sat up straight and rapped the desk sharply with a hamlike fist, then stood up. He moved across the room to the hat tree and got his hat, which he jammed down on his head. Then he hurried out of the building.

So Rusk tried again. He took with him five more deputies. On approaching Ned Christie's Fort, Rusk could see that Ned Christie had been busy. The woods behind the buildings had been cleared away, and there was no way to get anywhere near without being out in the open, exposed to the deadly accurate gunfire from the second-floor gun ports. Rusk called a halt. Dogs barked. Otherwise it was quiet. There was no one to be seen.

"He's ready for us," said Rusk in a quiet voice, "as usual."

The deputies had left their horses behind to approach on foot. A man named Joe Bowers was standing beside Rusk.

"Maybe no one's home," said Bowers.

"Oh, he's in there all right," said Rusk. "Him and more. They're just waiting for us to get close enough for a good shot. They're looking at us right now."

Rusk was right. Inside the house, Ned Christie was in the loft, and he was looking. Beside him was Youngbird. At other ports were the two Archies.

"Is that Rusk?" asked Ned Christie.

Youngbird looked, squinting his eyes.

"Yes," he said, "that's Rusk. The one in front."

"Do you know the others?" asked Ned.

Youngbird looked carefully, studying the faces as best he could from that distance.

"No," he said. "I don't know them."

They could see six men, Rusk standing more or less in the middle and a step or two in front of the other five. The other five were strung out in a line. Each man held a rifle in his right hand. Each man had at least one pistol strapped to his side or tucked in his belt. One man held something else in his hand. It was difficult to tell at that distance what it might be. It looked like a small bundle of sticks. Then Rusk suddenly shifted his rifle to his left hand and held up his right hand. He took a couple of steps forward. No one else moved.

"Ned Christie," he shouted.

No answer came from the fort.

"We know you're in there," called Rusk. "If you come out now, there won't be any shooting. We'll go to Fort Smith, and you'll get a fair trial."

Up in the loft Ned Christie's rifle had a bead on Rusk. But that would be too easy, too fast. Ned moved the rifle barrel half an inch to the left. The bead was on Bowers. He pulled the trigger. Bowers jerked and screamed. He dropped his rifle and staggered backwards. Rusk ran to him, grabbed him under the arms and started dragging him back toward the trees. The other deputies also turned and ran for the trees. The front door of the cabin flew open, and two Indian women and five small children emerged, running toward the woods. Someone inside the cabin jerked the door shut again.

"Look," said Charlie Copeland, one of the deputies who had just secured himself behind a large tree. Rusk looked up and saw the women and children running.

"Let them go," he said.

"Well, what now, Dave?" said Copeland.

Rusk looked around. Bowers was on the ground, bleeding badly from a chest wound. Rusk figured he wouldn't last long. Rusk had to make some sort of decision. His roving eyes stopped on an old wagon that was standing beside the shop.

"See that wagon over there?" he said.

"Yeah," said Copeland.

"You think a couple of you can make your way over there without getting hit?"

"Yeah. If y'all give us good cover fire."

"Okay, Charlie," said Rusk. "You and, uh, Milo get over there. The rest of us will shoot at them gunholes up there and give you some cover. Get over there and fill that wagon up with everything you can find that will burn. Set her on fire and shove her into the Fort. We'll burn them out."

Charlie Copeland and Milo Creekmore ran for the wagon. As they ran, the other deputies began firing at the gun ports of Ned Christie's Fort. There was no fire returned from the Fort. The two deputies reached the wagon, and they quickly piled dry brush and scraps of wood they found around the shop into the back of the wagon. When they thought they had enough flammable trash loaded, Copeland struck a match and held it to some of the dried brush. It took three matches, but he finally got a fire started.

"All right," he said, "let's get this thing aimed at the house."

Copeland and Creekmore pulled on the wagon until they got it aimed in the direction they wanted. Then they got behind it and ran, shoving. With a mighty final heave, they let the wagon go on its way. It was downhill to the Fort. They turned and ran back toward the safety of the trees, the rifle fire from their companions still providing them with cover. Creekmore and Copeland reached the trees about the time the wagon reached the fort. At the last minute, the wagon veered, and it just clipped the corner of the cabin, causing it to spin and break apart. The pile of trash and the pieces of wagon, some of them, burned harmlessly there beside their target. Back in the woods the deputies watched.

"Damn," said Copeland. "What now?"

"Fix a fuse to that dynamite," said Rusk. "We'll blow the damn place to hell."

Copeland picked up the bundle he had been carrying earlier in his left hand from the place behind a tree where he had deposited it for safety. He reached into his coat pocket and pulled out a coil of fuse. Unfolding a penknife, he cut the fuse and fixed a length of it to the bundle.

"That ought to be just about right," he said, holding it out straight for an eyeball measurement.

"I'll take it," said Fields, another of the deputies. "I've got a good throwing arm."

"All right," said Rusk. "Get ready. Charlie will light the fuse. You run, but don't get any closer than you have to to make a good throw. Pitch it, turn around, and head back."

"I got you," said Fields. He took the bundle in his right hand, balancing it up over his shoulder as if ready to throw.

"Ready?" said Charlie Copeland.

"I'm ready."

Copeland struck a match and lit the fuse.

"Go," he said, and the fuse started to fizz even as he spoke. Fields ran. He ran hard. He ran across the open space toward the cabin, and he hurled the missile with all his might. Just as he released it, a shot from one of the upstairs gun ports caught him in the left shoulder and spun him around. He dropped to his knees. Then he was back up, running for all he was worth, clutching his hurt shoulder, trailing blood behind him. The bundle of dynamite sticks hit the side wall of Ned Christie's Fort and rebounded separating itself from its fuse. It lay there harmlessly, as the fuse fizzled some feet away from it. Fields made his way back into the trees and dropped to the ground.

Rusk pulled a notepad from his pocket along with a pencil and started to scribble. He spoke to Creekmore as he wrote.

"Take this to Tahlequah," he said. "Send a wire to Marshal Yoes. Tell him we need help. We need it bad. Wait for an answer. Then get back here."

He tore the sheet off the pad and handed it to Creekmore, then stuck the pad and pencil back into his pocket. Creekmore didn't bother to reply. He took the sheet of paper and ran toward the horses. Rusk watched as Creekmore disappeared through the woods. Then he looked at Bowers and at Fields. Bowers was unconscious. Fields was still awake and obviously in great pain. Rusk didn't think that either man would live. He had not brought a wagon in which to haul away wounded. Nor had he brought enough men to spare anyone to go back with wounded. He had a tough decision to make: either maintain the siege of the fort and allow the two men to die there in the woods, or abandon the siege to try to get them to town for medical attention. Rusk knew that Judge Parker wanted Ned Christie in the worst possible way. He himself wanted to get Ned Christie. He decided that the two wounded deputies would probably not make it back to Tahlequah anyway. They would wait. They had Ned Christie penned up. They would wait.

But the wait proved to be extremely tedious. It seemed to Rusk that it was taking Creekmore an incredibly long period of time to get to Tahlequah, send a telegram, receive the reply, and get back. He knew he was wrong, but it seemed almost as if time were standing still. During the tense waiting period, Rusk and the two remaining able-bodied deputies there with him occasionally fired symbolic shots at Ned Christie's Fort. Someone occasionally fired shots back from inside. But there was hardly a real battle being waged. It was as if each party simply wanted to remind the other now and then of its presence.

At long last, Creekmore returned. He had the reply from Marshal Yoes, and as soon as he was close enough for Rusk to hear, he started talking.

"Yoes says stay here," he said. "Keep him in there. He says he's sending all the help we need."

Again it seemed like an interminable wait, but by the time the sun had set that evening, the number of deputies surrounding Ned Christie's home had increased to thirty. It was the largest posse yet assembled in the attempt to capture or kill Ned Christie, and Rusk thought for sure that he had him this time. But once again, he was doomed to disappointment. Perhaps it was the seeming impossibility of penetrating the walls of the fort. Perhaps it was the expanse of clearing that one had to venture into in order to get close to the fort, thereby exposing oneself to extreme danger from the deadly accurate rifle fire of Ned Christie and his companions. Perhaps it was simply the result of the demoralizing effect of watching the two deputies lying on the ground, bleeding, slowly dying. At any rate, when the sun began to light up the area the following morning. Rusk could see that his small army had no more stomach for the fight. It seemed hopeless, and they were ready to abandon the entire operation. He tried to tell them how important it was that they get Ned Christie, how badly Judge Parker wanted the man, what a dangerous outlaw Ned Christie was, that he was even an enemy of the United States and he needed to be brought to justice. None of it worked. The deputies began deserting. Finally Rusk, utterly frustrated, announced that the siege was over, and they left. Ned Christie had won again.

Chapter 16

You sent for me, sir?"

From behind his desk, Yoes flinched, startled at the voice. The voice was soft, low, warm, and liquid with a deep southern drawl. What had startled Yoes was the unexpectedness of the voice. He hadn't heard anyone approaching, no sound of footsteps, no opening or closing sounds from the big front door. But then he knew that Paden Tolbert was like that: a quiet, unassuming man who moved like a cat, smoothly and silently, a cold, calculating man with an absolutely even disposition, one who never acted on impulse but planned carefully, methodically, before making even the smallest move. Yoes sat up straight, trying to recover his dignity.

"Yes," he said. "Come in, Paden. Sit down."

Tolbert moved across the room, dropping his hat to the floor on its crown beside the chair there in front of Yoes's desk. He sat down and crossed one leg over the other. His every movement was smooth.

He seemed to make no noise. He sat calmly, politely, waiting for Yoes to call the shots.

"Paden," said the head marshal, "I sent for you because I want to put you in charge of this Ned Christie thing. Nothing we've done has worked. It's been handled badly. Dave Rusk went out there and had Ned Christie surrounded with thirty men. They came away empty-handed. I'm putting you in charge. You plan the operation. You take however many men you want. You pick them. You take whatever equipment and supplies you want. Do it your way, and don't worry about the expense. I just want it done, and I want it done right, and I want it done soon."

"All right," said Tolbert. "It will take me a few days to get ready."

"I figured that," said Yoes.

"You got a file on this case?"

"Right here." Yoes handed a folder across the desk to Tolbert.

"I'll need somebody who's been there," said Tolbert.

"Dave Rusk is in town," said Yoes. "He's been out there several times."

"Good," said Tolbert. "I'll run him down."

He reached down and picked his hat up off of the floor, depositing it on his head in one smooth move, and almost before Yoes knew it, he was out of the office without having made another sound. Yoes stood up, his mouth opened. He thought about calling after Tolbert. Somehow he felt like the interview had not ended. He wasn't sure he had said every-

thing that needed to be said, but he couldn't think
of what else he might have needed to tell Tolbert. It
had been such a short conversation, but clearly Tolbert thought that he had heard everything he needed
to hear. He would take it from there. Yoes dropped
back into his chair and heaved a sigh of relief. He
probably wouldn't hear anything more from Tolbert
until it was all over and done.

Paden Tolbert returned to the small house on the
outskirts of Fort Smith that he shared with his
younger brother John. John had known that Paden
had been summoned to the marshal's office, and he
was waiting anxiously for the news. He met his
brother at the door.

"Well," he said, "what is it?"

"We're going after Ned Christie," said the elder
Tolbert.

"What did I tell you?" said John. "I knew it. I
knew it. Are you in charge?"

"Yeah," said Paden.

"Hot damn," said John. "And we'll get him, too."

"I've got to read this file here," said Paden.
"While I do that, I want you to go find Dave Rusk
for me. You know Dave."

"Yeah, I know him."

"Bring him over here for a talk. He's in town
somewhere."

"I'll get him," said John. "Be right back here with
him."

By the time John returned with Rusk, Paden Tolbert already had several pages of notes made and several lists: one of supplies, the rest were lists of names, five or six names on each list. He had also listed by date the next several days. Under each date was a location and a note of something to be accomplished. Specific times were noted under some of the dates. Spread out on the table before him was a map of western Arkansas and the Indian Territory. He stood up when John came into the house with Rusk.

"Hello, Dave," he said. "Thanks for coming."

"Howdy, Paden. John here says that the old man gave you the Ned Christie case."

"That's right, Dave," said Tolbert, "and I need your help. I've never been there, and you have."

Tolbert could tell that Rusk was working to cover up his embarrassment at having been replaced. He had anticipated that, and he tried his best to avoid aggravating that embarrassment.

"Can you locate Ned Christie's house for me on this map?" he said.

Rusk stepped over to examine the map. After a minute or so, he stuck a finger on it.

"Be right about here," he said.

Tolbert drew an *X* on the map where Rusk had put his finger.

"All right," he said. "Any landmarks along this road to tell me when I get there?"

"Well, yeah," said Rusk, "but it would be a whole lot easier if I was to just go along with you and show you the way."

"I want you to meet me here," said Tolbert, jabbing his finger at the road near where he had drawn the X. "That means I have to be able to find it by myself. I've got something else for you to do in the meantime. That is, if you're willing to go along."

"Sure," said Rusk. "I'll go along."

The next day Paden Tolbert was riding the train from Fort Smith to Clarksville, Arkansas, in the company of Wes Bowman. Bowman's name had been at the top of Tolbert's first list of names. There were five men in Clarksville that Tolbert wanted for his posse. He and Bowman were going there to meet with them and try to recruit them for the posse. He had left with brother John another list of names of men to be recruited in Fort Smith during his absence, and he had personally recruited Cap White before having left for Clarksville. He had given White the list of supplies to gather, and instructions on where to have them delivered. Rusk's assignment had been to take care of a special order from Coffeeville, Kansas.

The following morning, early, Tolbert and Bowman were back on the train. They were headed back to Fort Smith, and with them were five other men, all the men on Tolbert's Clarksville list. No one had turned Tolbert down. At Fort Smith, John Tolbert met them at the station. He had been equally successful, having recruited the four men on the list his brother had left with him. That brought the total to fourteen. Cap White was also waiting at the depot with the supplies he had gathered. After a short layover, the train that had brought Tolbert, Bowman, and the five other men from Clarksville would pull out again, heading west to West Fork, Arkansas. The deputies all pitched in to get the supplies loaded onto the train. It was a short, sixty-mile ride by rail, and soon they were at West Fork. There Paden Tolbert found Sheriff Gus York waiting for him at the station.

"I guess Dave Rusk found you all right," he said.

"Yes, sir," said York, "and we've got everything you wanted right here."

Tolbert saw a wagon hitched to a team of mules standing not far from where he and York were talking.

"That for me?" he asked.

"That's yours," said York.

Tolbert turned to his younger brother.

"John," he said, "get our supplies loaded into this wagon."

"Right," said John, and he gathered up the rest of the posse and set to work, leaving Tolbert alone with York.

"What about the horses?" said Tolbert.

"I've got them lined up," said York. "All you need."

"What about that shipment from Coffeeville?"

"It came in last night on the train," said York. "It's waiting for you right over there. Inside."

He jerked a thumb over his shoulder toward the station house.

"Let's take a look," said Tolbert, and he and York walked over to the building. York led the way inside. He nodded to the express agent as he passed him by on his way to the rear of the building. There was a large double door, like a barn door, large enough to drive a wagon through. There just inside the door was what Tolbert was looking for: a small field cannon with a four-foot barrel mounted on a heavy wooden carriage. Wooden crates beside the cannon held forty bullet-shaped projectiles. Tolbert nodded his head slowly to indicate his pleasure. Then he pointed at the big doors.

"I take it we can drive the wagon around and load it up through here," he said.

"Yes, sir," said York.

Tolbert went back out to the train where his men were still loading supplies into the wagon.

"Polk," he called.

The one black man in the bunch turned in response.

"Yes, sir?"

"They can finish up here without you. You go on ahead and get the groceries."

"Yes, sir."

Polk took off, and Tolbert called out to his brother.

"John," he said, "when you get done here, have someone drive the wagon around to the far side of the station house there. You'll see a couple of big loading doors. Stop it there."

"Okay," said John.

"Gus," said Tolbert, turning back to York, "there's thirteen of us here. One man will drive the wagon. Can you have twelve horses saddled and brought around?"

"Sure," said York. "You want them now?"

"We'll be ready to head out right soon," said Tolbert.

"I'll bring them along then," said York, and he hurried away. Just then Tolbert heard the sound of approaching horses' hooves, and he turned to see five mounted men riding toward him. As they got closer, he recognized them: George Jefferson and Mack Peel and Mills and Burkett. They were all deputies. The fifth rider was young Sam Maples. The riders reined in their mounts a few feet away from Tolbert. Tolbert nodded a slow greeting.

"We heard you was going after Ned Christie," said Peel. "We come to join up with you."

"I got plenty of men," said Tolbert.

"You got to let me go," said Sam Maples. "He killed my father. I'm Sam Maples. Dan Maples's son."

"I know who you are, boy," said Tolbert. "That's the problem. I don't need anyone along who's all emotional and bent on revenge. And I do need men with experience. This is work for cool heads."

"It's been over four years, Mr. Tolbert," said Sam. "I've calmed down."

"He's a good man, Paden," said Jefferson. "He deserves this. And me and Mack were with him when Dan got shot. Take us along. All of us."

Tolbert studied the three men a moment. Silently he wished that young Maples had stayed at home. He was afraid that he would regret this decision.

"All right," he said. "Give these boys here a hand then."

Now, with Rusk still planning to meet them later, the total number in the posse would be nineteen.

They went on that evening to Summer's Store, which was just by the border. There they were joined by four more volunteers. It became obvious to Paden Tolbert that his attempts to keep his mission secret had failed. They spent the night, rested, ate well, and the following morning, Tolbert took advantage of this, his last opportunity to instruct his charges.

"We're going to leave out of here in a few minutes," he said. "We'll head out single file. The wagon will come along last. I want everyone to keep quiet. When we camp tonight, we're going to be right close to Ned Christie. There'll be no talking. No fires. No noise made. Everyone will get a good night's sleep, and we'll be up at four o'clock tomorrow morning to move in. Are there any questions?"

There were none, and the posse, now numbering twenty-three, crossed the border into the Cherokee Nation, heading for the home of Ned Christie.

Chapter 17

It was a cold November night, not bitter cold, but crisp, not nearly so cold as a night in *nuhdadewi*, the big trading month, might have been. Ned Christie sat outside alone. There was a full moon, and so it was not a dark night. The stars were bright in the clear sky. He could see the place where the dog ran, and he could see *anichuja*, the boys. He saw also the group that goes west in the winter and the lone bright one, the one that you see early in the morning. He stared at the big round moon, and he thought back over the previous twenty-six or so hours. They had started at just about sundown the night before, there at *gatiyuo-i*, the stomp ground. It was a little late in the year for a stomp dance, but the weather was mild. They had danced all night, moving in counter-clockwise circles around the sacred fire, the fire that was said to have been kept perpetually burning, that had been carried west over the Trail of Tears, over *digejiluhstanuh*, the way they were

herded down there away from where they wanted
to be.

They danced a cycle of dances throughout the
night, following the leader, singing the songs with
him, to the rhythm of turtle-shell rattles strapped to
the calves of women. One of the shell-shakers was
Ned Christie's wife, and Ned Christie was proud of
her. Arch Christie was there too, and so was Young
Archie Wolf. And they danced and they sang, until
the sun came out again in the morning.

Then the women began laying out a great feast,
and the ball players gathered around the thirty-foot-
high pole with the carved fish on top. The men who
would play carried their ball sticks, made of hickory
or pecan, about two-and-one-half-feet long, bent at
one end and laced there to form a racket. The women
would play with bare hands, playing against the
men. Ned played ball, and so did Gatey and the two
Archies. Once when Ned had the ball clamped securely between the rackets of his two sticks and was
just about to make a toss at the fish for a point, Gatey
grabbed him from behind and threw him off balance.
He missed the target, and a woman picked up the
ball and threw it and scored. Another time, when
Archie Christie had the ball, Ned thought that Gatey
moved just a bit slowly on purpose. Arch made his
toss and hit the mark. In the end, as usual, the
women won the game.

Then they had feasted well, and they had visited,
and sometime in the early afternoon, they had begun
leaving for their homes. Archie Wolf had accompanied the Christies, having told his own parents he

would see them sometime later. So the sun was down again, and while Ned Christie sat outside alone gazing at the sky, Gatey and both Archies were in the house. The two young men, Ned thought, were probably eating again. He thought about going back inside and having a bite himself before putting himself to bed for the night. It had been a long time without sleep, but the day and the night before had been good. He was glad that the weather had allowed the activity to take place so late in the season. He was glad to have had that experience one last time. He stood up, took a deep breath of the fresh, cool air, and walked into the house.

As he had expected, the two Archies were seated at the table. Gatey was busy at the cupboard. Ned walked to the stove and checked the pan there. There was still hot coffee. He got a cup, poured himself some, and carried it to the table. He sat down and was reaching for a piece of the good corn bread there when they heard the dogs.

It was not a menacing bark, as if the dogs had sensed some intruder in their territory. It was not the deep-throated baying of the hounds on the trail of a rabbit or a raccoon or some other creature of the woods. Rather it was a cacophony of whines and whimpers, accompanied by scratching at the door. These were not house dogs, had not ever, in fact, been inside the house. Ned turned to face the door. His face showed a calm resignation. Gatey and the two Archies also stopped still and listened. No one spoke. The two Archies looked at each other. Then Arch Christie looked up toward his mother. She was staring at the door. Ned picked up the piece of corn bread he had reached for. He ate the corn bread and drank his coffee in silence. By the time he had finished, the dogs had stopped their whining and gone their ways. Ned stood up, walked to the door, opened it, and went outside.

He walked into his shop, found the lantern in the dark, lit it, and turned up the light. Then he located a pair of shears. He rejected them and found another pair. He tested their edge. Then he took them to his grinding stone and sharpened them. He tested the edge again. He reached back behind his head with his left hand and gathered up his long hair. Then with the shears in his right, he reached back to cut. Carefully he placed the shorn locks on a clean corner of his work table. Then he cut some more.

Inside the house, Arch Christie spoke in an apprehensive voice.

"Mother?" he said.

"Check all the guns," said Archie Wolf.

"And the water barrel," said Gatey. "We must be ready."

Out in the shop Ned Christie gathered up all the locks of hair he had cut from his head, and he folded them up in an oil cloth. He stuck the oil cloth inside his shirt and went to a corner of the shop for a shovel. With the shovel in one hand and the lantern in the other, he walked into the woods. He dug the hole deep, and down in the bottom of the hole, he placed the folded oil cloth containing the hair. He replaced the dirt, patted it down, and smoothed it and covered it with leaves. Then he went to the creek.

Back inside the house later, Ned found that the others had already prepared everything. Well, almost everything. He got out his best suit and his white shirt, and he laid them out carefully. Gatey and the two Archies stared at Ned, briefly; a long stare would have been impolite. He looked quite a bit different with his hair cropped short. He looked somehow shorter and stockier. And he seemed to look a different age. Was it older or younger? They couldn't decide. He looked different. No one said anything, not about the dogs, and not about the hair.

Chapter 18

Wes Bowman put a hand on Paden Tolbert's shoulder and gave a gentle shove. Tolbert moaned low, rolled his head to one side, and opened his eyes.

"Four o'clock, Paden," said Bowman in a voice that was not much more than a harsh whisper.

"Wake the others," said Tolbert. "Remind everyone to keep quiet. We'll be moving out in a half an hour."

Tolbert tossed aside his top blanket and sat up, feeling the crisp morning air. He reached for the fresh pair of socks he had laid out handy the night before and pulled them on. Then he pulled on his boots, and he stood up to stretch. He pulled a clean shirt on over his head and tucked the tail into his trousers. He put his hat on his head, pulling it down tight. Then he put on his vest. He thought about putting on the jacket but decided against it. Once the sun came out, the chill would be burned from the air, and in the meantime, it would help to keep him

alert. Tolbert carried two six-guns, but he had only
one holster. He strapped on the gunbelt from which
the holster depended, and he stuck the second six-
gun in the waistband of his trousers. He rolled up
his bedroll behind the saddle. He shoved his Winchester into the saddle boot. He was ready to go. He
glanced around and saw that the whole camp was
slowly coming to life.

The men went about their business in silence.
They needed no instructions from Tolbert. He had
detailed his plan to them the night before, well before they had arrived at the campsite. They all knew
what was expected of them. Each man knew what
to do. As soon as they were all up, dressed, packed,
and had their horses saddled, Tolbert mounted his
horse. Dave Rusk climbed into the saddle and rode
up alongside Tolbert. Tolbert watched while the rest
of the men got mounted. Then he gave Rusk a nod.
Rusk started riding slowly, and Tolbert followed
him. One by one, the others fell in line until they
had formed a long single file. At last the wagon lum-
bered forward to take up the rear.

Gatey woke up to the smell of coffee. Ned was already up and dressed. Perhaps he had not slept at
all. He was sitting at the table with a cup of coffee,
and he was wearing the black suit. He looked, she
thought, as if he were preparing to go to Tahlequah
for a council meeting. But his hair was short. She
got up and dressed and started to prepare breakfast.
Soon the two Archies began to stir. No one spoke.
There was something ominous hanging in the air.

Young Archie Wolf climbed down from the loft where he had slept. He had on only his trousers. His hair was tousled from sleep, and his eyes were still about half closed. He walked to the front door, opened it, and stepped outside. The early morning ground was cold beneath his bare feet. He had taken but two or three steps away from the door when he heard the sharp crack, and not more than three feet away from him, off to his right, bits of dirt and rock were splattered by the sudden impact of a rifle bullet. He felt some of the flying particles of earth sting into the side of his leg. Suddenly wide awake, he turned and ran back to the door. Inside the house he slammed the door behind him. Ned Christie was up in an instant. He shoved Archie out of the way, and dropped the heavy bar into place to secure the door. The fight was on.

Ned climbed up into the loft and moved from one gunport to another. He could see right away that he was completely surrounded. Young Archie Wolf followed Ned back up into the loft. Arch Christie was still up there. The three men each took a position at a gun port and returned fire, but as soon as they did, the woods all around the house seemed to come alive. Gatey paused for an instant, but only for an instant. She went back to her work. The roar from the woods was constant. There seemed to be no space between gunshots.

Out in the woods. Paden Tolbert touched Wes Bowman on the shoulder. Bowman leaned toward Tolbert to listen as Tolbert spoke.

"Pass the word along," said Tolbert, "to ease up. We've made our point. Now we're just wasting shells."

Gradually the firing died down, and Tolbert issued new instructions.

"Don't waste your shots," he said. "Shoot if you think you've got a good target, and shoot back whenever they shoot, but don't just throw buckets full of lead at them."

Tolbert walked back through the woods to the place where the wagon waited. There a fire was going, and the smell of fresh coffee and frying bacon filled the air.

"If you got any hungry men," said the cook, "I'm ready for them."

"I'll get them started," said Tolbert.

Tolbert had deployed the posse in two groups. There was an inner circle, surrounding the cabin, and an outer circle. The purpose of the outer circle was to keep anyone else from coming to the aid of Ned Christie, to catch anyone who might possibly escape from the cabin and somehow get through the first circle, and to serve as a relief for those men on the front line. Tolbert told the men in the outer circle to start going back to eat, every other man. When a man finished his meal, he was to relieve someone in the inner circle. They would keep this up until everyone had eaten. Tolbert had not allowed fires at the campsite for fear that they might alert Ned Christie to the posse's presence. He had planned to surround Ned Christie's Fort early in the morning to catch the occupants totally by surprise. With everything in place just as he wanted it, there was no hurry. Now let all these men get their bellies full.

From his post up in the loft inside the cabin, Ned Christie saw that Gatey had spread the food on the table. He looked over at his son and nodded his head.

"Go on," he said. "Eat."

"Archie," said Arch Christie. "You go first."

Archie Wolf put down the gun he held and went down to the main floor to eat. When he was done, Arch Christie would take his turn. Then Ned would eat. That way there would be two men at the gunports at all times. Ned watched the woods for any movement, any activity he might detect. Now and then he could see a little but never very much. This posse, he thought, was not acting like the previous ones. This posse was not being led by Rusk. Whoever was out there, whoever had brought those men in before sunrise, whoever had positioned them out there, whoever was telling them what to do and what not to do, he was a smarter man than Rusk.

Things were pretty quiet until about mid-morning. Young Archie Wolf, watching through his gun port, saw a deputy in the woods carelessly partially expose himself from his hiding place behind a tree. Young Archie drew a careful bead and fired. He nicked the deputy's arm. The shot was answered by a barrage from the woods. The three defenders huddled down beneath their gun ports and waited for the onslaught to subside. Eventually it did, and they fired a few random shots back at the posse to let them know that they were still there.

Out in the woods Paden Tolbert was standing between Wes Bowman and Dave Rusk.

"We're getting nowhere like this," he said.

"That fort is two logs thick all the way around," said Rusk. "No bullet's going to go through that."

"And even if we shoot into them gun ports," said Bowman, "our bullets ain't getting through. You'd have to be up in a tree straight in line with one of them things with walls that thick and that slot being so narrow as it is. All we're doing is shooting into the walls again. We might hit them with splinters. Might."

"Wes," said Tolbert, "run around and gather up about a half a dozen of the boys who are carrying old muzzle loaders. Bring them over here."

Bowman hesitated, looking as if he'd like to further question that peculiar order. Instead he said, "Okay," and he turned and hurried off to do as he'd been told. Tolbert then turned to Dave Rusk.

"Dave," he said, "go back to the wagon. There's a bundle of sticks in there and there's a bundle of rags. There's also a can of coal oil. Fetch it all down here."

Tolbert reached into his vest pocket for the box of machine-rolled Sweet Caps and took out a cigarette. He put the box back in his pocket and got a match. He struck it on his boot sole and lit the cigarette. Then he leaned against the tree, peering around to watch the house as he smoked and waited.

Two men with muzzle-loading rifles came running up to stand beside him.

"Wes said you wanted us over here," said one of the men. "What is it?"

"Just hold on until we're all together here," said Tolbert. He took a long drag on his cigarette. In another couple of minutes, there were six men with muzzle loaders gathered around, and Bowman had returned. Then Dave Rusk came trotting back down, a bundle of sticks and a bundle of rags under one arm and the coal oil can in his other hand. He put the stuff down on the ground beside Tolbert.

"All right, boys," said Tolbert. "Load up with everything except the lead. You're going to shoot these sticks."

"What?" said one of the men.

"You heard me right," said Tolbert reaching down to rip off a strip of rag.

"I'm already all loaded up," said the man.

"Me too," said another.

"You know how to get that lead out of there?" said Bowman.

"No," said the rifleman.

"Point your gun at that house yonder, preferably at one of them gunports," said Bowman, "and pull the trigger."

"Oh," said the man. He took aim and fired. The other riflemen with loaded rifles also fired their shots at the house. Then they began to reload. This time without the lead. Tolbert had taken the piece of rag and wrapped it tightly around one end of one of the sticks, all of which had been cut to lengths of about three feet. He held the stick out toward Rusk.

"Slop some coal oil on this rag, Dave," he said.

Rusk picked up the can and poured some coal oil onto the rag. Tolbert turned to the nearest rifleman.

"You ready?" he said.

"Yes, sir."

Tolbert stuck the stick into the rifle barrel, struck a match and lit the rag.

"Shoot," he said.

The deputy aimed at the house and fired. The flaming stick flew threw the air. Its flight was wobbly, but it reached the house and bounced off of the log wall to fall to the ground and burn harmlessly.

"It works," said Bowman.

"Load them all up like that," said Tolbert. "If we can set that thing on fire they'll have to come out."

The next stick flew far off target. Two more bounced off the wall. One landed on the roof, but it burned itself out without igniting the roof. A couple of the sticks lost their flames in flight, tumbled end over end and drifted way off target. They loaded up a second round and tried again.

"Hey," said Arch Christie. "What are they doing?"

"They're shooting flaming arrows at us," said Archie Wolf.

"If they were real arrows," said Ned, "they'd fly straight. They're shooting sticks out of their rifles."

Archie Wolf watched the wobbling flight of the next stick. It went far off to the right. He laughed.

"Yes," he said. "They'd do much better with real bows and arrows."

Regular gunshots were few and far between. Under the instructions of Paden Tolbert, the members of the posse stayed well hidden. They were taking no unnecessary chances. And Tolbert had earlier determined that gunshots at the fort were almost useless. They continued to fire the flaming sticks at the house until midday. Then Tolbert gave that idea up, too. Back at the wagon, the cook had prepared the noon meal, and again the posse ate in shifts. When Tolbert took his turn to eat, he noticed a small crowd of Indians gathered not far away.

"What the hell is that?" he said.

"I don't know, Mr. Tolbert," said Frank Polk. "They just kind of ambled in here a while back. Just watching, I guess. I don't see no weapons."

Dave Rusk was sitting on the ground a few feet away eating.

"That old man over there," he said. "That's old Watt Christie. That's Ned Christie's daddy."

"You know him?" said Tolbert.

"Yeah, I know him," said Rusk.

"He know you?"

"Yeah, he knows who I am."

Tolbert stared at Watt Christie there in the small group of Indians. He thought for a moment. Then he walked over beside where Dave Rusk sat, and he squatted on his haunches.

"As soon as you finish eating," he said, "I want you to go over there and have a talk with Ned Christie's daddy. See if you can get him to talk to his boy. See if he'll do what he can to talk him into giving up. Tell him we don't want to kill him. We don't want to kill anybody. We're just doing our duty as lawmen. We want to take him to Fort Smith for a fair trial. Tell him he can put a stop to all this, if he'll just go talk to his boy. Tell him if he'll do that, we won't shoot, nobody out here will shoot while they're talking. Can you do that, Dave?"

"Yeah. All right," said Rusk. "I'll give it a try."

A few feet away, leaning against a wagon wheel, young Sam Maples sat with a plate of food. He listened while Tolbert spoke to Rusk, and he did not like what he heard. He scowled, but he kept quiet. Tolbert had not wanted him along in the first place. He finished his meal in silence and went back into the woods to his post.

When Tolbert sat down to eat, Rusk had finished, and he walked over to the small gathering of Indians. They were too far away for Tolbert to hear what was going on. He ate his meal. In a few minutes, Rusk returned. He was shaking his head as he approached Tolbert.

"No luck?" said Tolbert.

"Hell, no," said Rusk. "The old bastard even pretended that he couldn't understand me. I know he can talk English. Hell, I've talked to him before. Another Indian interpreted for him. Anyhow, he says he won't do it. He don't trust us. And even if he did trust us, he says that Ned Christie won't ever surrender, no matter what. It would be a waste of time for him to go talk."

"Well," said Tolbert, "we tried. There's only one thing I can think of for us to do now."

"What's that?" said Rusk.

Tolbert slowly turned his head toward the wagon. There in the wagon bed, the forty-pound cannon sat gleaming in the sunlight.

Chapter 19

Paden Tolbert stepped out into the clearing a few feet. Inside the cabin, Arch Christie took aim with his rifle.

"Don't shoot," said Ned. "He wants to talk. Let him."

Tolbert shouted Ned's name. Ned did not answer. He waited to see what the man had to say. Tolbert called out again.

"Ned Christie," he said. "I know you can hear me in there. I want you to come out and surrender. My name is Paden Tolbert. I'm a deputy United States marshal. I don't want to have to kill you. I want you to stand trial. But I am prepared to stay here for as long as it takes to see this thing through. It'd be a whole lot better for everyone if you'd just give up. If you come out, you or anyone else in there with you, we won't shoot. You got my word on that."

Tolbert stood alone, an easy target. He waited for some response from the Fort, but there was none.

From back in the woods, Dave Rusk forced out a harsh whisper.

"Paden," he said, "get back here before he decides to kill you."

Tolbert turned around calmly and started walking back toward the trees. He was not quite so calm and unconcerned inside as he appeared to be, but he did figure that he was safer walking than running. If he turned and ran for cover, he thought, he might have drawn fire. But somehow he couldn't picture Ned Christie, even though he had never met the man, putting a bullet into the back of a man who was calmly walking away. He knew that Ned Christie had been accused of doing exactly that to Dan Maples a little more than four years ago, but he had also read the reports of the fights that had taken place between Ned Christie and the deputies since then. Whatever the truth, Tolbert walked back into the trees unhurt. No shots had been fired.

"You boys ready with that thing?" he asked

From the loft, Ned saw Paden Tolbert walk away. He put down his rifle, and he looked down at Gatey who had just finished preparing a noon meal.

"Keep watching, boys," he said.

He climbed down from the loft and walked to her. He put his hands on her shoulders and looked into her eyes for a brief moment. Then he held her close.

"I want you to go," he said.

"I should stay with you," she said.

"No. It's time for you to go now."

Then a loud blast shattered the silence. It was like

a shot, but it was also like thunder. And a moment after the roar, something thudded hard into the side of the house.

"What was that?" said Arch Christie.

"Galogwe-equa," said Young Archie Wolf. "A cannon."

Ned ran to the front door with Gatey. He jerked off the bar and opened the door.

"Go," he said.

She hesitated. She looked from her husband to her son.

"Go on, Mother," said Arch. "We're staying."

Gatey turned and ran, and Ned shut the door and barred it again. Then he climbed back up into the loft.

"Damn," said Dave Rusk. "Did you see that damn thing just bounce off the wall?"

"Load her up and try it again," said Tolbert.

Then he saw the woman coming out of the house.

"Hold your fire," he shouted. "Let her get clear."

He turned back to the men at the cannon.

"Go on and reload," he said. "Get it ready."

Tolbert watched as Gatey ran into the woods to safety. Then he turned to his cannon crew.

"Go ahead," he said. "Fire."

The match was touched to the fuse, and the cannon roared and belched black smoke. The big bullet-shaped projectile went hurtling through the air. It came down at a sharp angle, stabbing itself into a log on the wall of Ned Christie's Fort. It stuck there for just an instant. Then its own weight pulled it loose and it fell to the ground. The only damage done to the fort was a gouge in one log. Tolbert heard a rustling of leaves to his right, and he turned to see Charlie Copeland approaching, his right hand holding the woman by her left arm.

"This here is Ned Christie's wife," said Copeland.

The woman looked at the ground.

"We ain't going to hurt you," said Paden Tolbert. "Will you tell us who all is in the house."

Still she stared at the ground. She did not answer.

"Do you understand English?" said Tolbert.

She did not answer.

"Hell," said Copeland, "she talks English as good as you and me."

Tolbert looked at her, but she still stared at the ground.

"Is that right?" he said. She did not answer. "Take her on back there where her daddy-in-law is waiting with them other folks, Charlie," said Tolbert, "and let her go."

"Let her go?" said Copeland.

"Charlie," said Tolbert, "we're fixing to kill the lady's husband here. Do you think we need to torment her any more than that? Go on now."

Copeland led Gatey away. The cannon crew was busy resighting the cannon. They had to do this after each shot because the big gun bucked so when it was fired. With the cannon realigned and reloaded, the crew looked toward Tolbert.

"Well, go on," he said. "Hit him again."

They fired again, and again they struck the fort, again with no effect.

"We ain't doing no good with that thing, Paden," said Bowman.

"Well," said Tolbert, "we brought forty rounds. If we hammer that wall enough, maybe it will give. Keep her going. I'm going to go back and have me a cup of java."

He walked back to the wagon, and Frank Polk poured him a hot cup of coffee. Heck Thomas was there with a cup.

"This is the damndest thing I've ever seen" said Thomas.

"Yeah," said Tolbert.

He looked over at the group of Indians who were waiting there and watching. He saw that Ned Christie's wife was standing beside her father-in-law. The group had grown larger by about half since last he had looked at them.

"How many men you reckon he's got in there with him?" said Thomas.

"Aw," said Tolbert, "I'd say no more than two more. Ned Christie and two more. That's my guess."

"That's what I'd say," said Thomas. "And how many of us are there?"

"Twenty-three," said Tolbert. "That's counting Frank here."

"I ain't never seen nothing like this," said Thomas. "No, sir. We must have shot over a thousand rounds at them. And all them—fire sticks. Now this cannon. And we ain't no closer to him than we were when we got here. I've never seen anything like it."

"That's one hell of a man in there," said Tolbert,

"but we're going to get him. One way or another. It's our job."

It was getting late. The sun was already low in the sky. Paden Tolbert was back at the cannon. He noticed that there were but three rounds left.

"Boys," he said, "we got to hit that wall a little bit harder. Pour some extra powder in there this time."

They loaded the cannon up again, this time with an extra charge of powder. They dropped the projectile into the barrel and rammed it home. They jostled the cannon back into position, taking careful aim, and they lit the fuse. There was a blinding flash and a tremendous roar. There were screams. One deputy's shirt was on fire. Two others threw him to the ground and rolled him over to put the flames out. The air was foul with the stench of burned black powder and thick with black smoke. Men were coughing. At least one man was groaning.

"Shit," said Paden Tolbert. It was the first time he had lost his composure. He quickly regained it though. "Who's hurt?" he said.

"Oh, I'm burnt some," said the man whose shirt had been on fire.

"Can you get back to the wagon all right? Do you need any help?" said Tolbert.

"No. I can make it all right."

"Well, go on back there then. Frank will have something to put on that. Go on."

The smoke had cleared a little, and Wes Bowman was standing beside the cannon.

"Well," he said, "that's the end of that."

Tolbert walked over to stand beside Bowman. He looked at the cannon. The barrel was split.

"I said to use more powder," he said "and they did."

He walked over to lean against a tree and stare at the cabin. It loomed there almost unharmed. The yard around it was littered with spent rounds fired from the cannon. Other than that, it did not even look like it had been under serious attack. Close by the cabin was the smaller and less substantial shop building. Off to the side of the shop was what appeared to be a scrap yard. There was a piece of an old wagon there. Tolbert looked back over his shoulder, and his eye caught Dave Rusk standing there.

"Dave," he said, "come here a minute."

Rusk walked over to stand beside Tolbert.

"Do you see that piece of wagon over yonder?" said Tolbert.

"Yeah," said Rusk. "It looks like what's left of one we busted up here a while back."

"It's kind of hard to tell from here," said Tolbert, "but it looks to me like the rear wheels and axle are pretty much together. Still some wood on it too."

"Yeah," said Rusk.

"Wait for the sun to go down," said Tolbert. "You think you can take a couple of men over there and get that thing?"

"Sure," said Rusk.

"What I'm wanting," said Tolbert, "is a shield. A rolling shield. If that thing ain't got enough wood on it, haul out some scrap with it. What I want is something two or three men can get behind to get up close to the house. You follow me?"

"Yeah," said Rusk. "I think so."

"Okay, but wait until it's dark before you make your move."

Tolbert reached into his pocket for a Sweet Caps as Rusk moved off to recruit his helpers.

By midnight they had finished the rolling shield, a wall of heavy planks attached to an axle and two wheels and a wagon tongue. They had worked on it back by their own wagon by the light of the fire where Frank Polk kept boiling fresh coffee. Men were sleeping as they had eaten, in shifts. The two circles surrounding the cabin were still in place. Paden Tolbert lifted the wagon tongue and tested the new device. He pushed it forward and pulled it back. He turned it around. It was manageable. He called Charlie Copeland to him, and they walked over to their supply wagon. Tolbert reached over the side and pulled back a canvas to reveal a box of dynamite sticks.

"How many of these do you think it will take to blow out that wall, Charlie?" he said.

"That's hard to say," said Copeland.

Tolbert gathered six sticks and held them up in a bundle.

"Will this do it?" he said.

"God almighty, Paden," said Copeland, "if that don't do it, I don't know what will."

"You want to tie them up then and fix a fuse?" said Tolbert, handing the sticks to Copeland.

"Sure thing."

Tolbert walked to the fire for another cup of coffee. He could see the gathered onlookers off in the distance. It was hard to tell in the dark just how many were over there, but he was pretty sure the numbers had increased even more. They were huddled in three groups around three small fires. He thought that he could make out Ned Christie's wife and father standing near the fire in the middle, but he wasn't sure. Wes Bowman appeared at the fire by Tolbert, poured himself a cup of coffee, and squatted down.

"We're getting us a sizeable audience over there," he said.

"Yeah," said Tolbert. "This thing has got to be brought to an end real soon now."

Bowman took a sip of coffee.

"It's going to start getting cold here pretty soon," he said.

"Yeah," said Tolbert. "Listen, Wes. Soon as you finish your coffee, I want you to round up Dave Rusk and two or three boys with good repeating rifles. Bring them up here. We got to make some plans."

Wes Bowman carrying his rifle and Charlie Copeland carrying the bundle of prepared dynamite sticks crouched low behind the makeshift shield. Paden Tolbert glanced to his right and left where the riflemen had been placed.

"You boys ready?" he said.

"We're ready," said one.

"Yes, sir," said the other.

Tolbert lifted the wagon tongue and looked out over the top of the shield toward Ned Christie's fort. It was nearly morning but still dark. Tolbert wanted the cover of darkness. He did not, however, want that same cover to be afforded the defenders of the fort for an extended period of time after the blast.

"All right," he said. "Let's go."

He gave a shove and started running, pushing the shield ahead of himself: The shield rolled. Bowman and Copeland ran along in a crouch behind it. The riflemen started firing at the gun ports as fast as they could. Tolbert ran behind the heavy shield, which had picked up speed on its own. He held fast to the wagon tongue. He couldn't let it get away from him. He had to look over the top of the shield now and then to check their direction. He had to steer with the wagon tongue. As they got closer to the cabin, the ground began to level off, and the speed of the shield decreased. They rolled up beside the shop, and Bowman turned sharply and ran to take a position there behind the building. They rolled on up closer to the cabin, almost touching the cabin with the shield before they stopped. Copeland jumped out from behind the shield and jammed the bundle of dynamite sticks underneath the bottom log of the wall. He struck a match and lit the fuse, and he jumped back behind the shield.

"Let's go," he said.

He grabbed the wagon tongue and helped Tolbert pull backward. They ran. The riflemen were still firing from the woods, but about halfway across the clearing, Tolbert and Copeland were aware that someone in the fort was returning fire. One or two slugs thudded into the shield. They ran. It was uphill as they got closer to the woods, and they had to pull harder. Then they were no longer running. They were pulling slowly uphill. Tolbert looked over his shoulder and saw the safety of the woods not too far away.

"Hell," he said, "drop this damn thing and run for it."

They turned loose of the wagon tongue and ran. Tolbert lost sight of Copeland. Just as he dived head-long for cover, he heard the incredible, deafening blast behind him.

Chapter 20

Tolbert hit the ground rolling. He came up to a sitting position and looked toward the cabin. Dust and debris and smoke filled the air around the site of the explosion. Here and there little flickering fires could be seen through the haze.

"Where's Charlie?" Tolbert shouted.

"Over here, Paden," Copeland answered. "I'm all right. Do you think them six sticks done the trick?"

"By God," said Tolbert. "They did it."

He stood up slowly and walked over to lean against a big tree and study the devastation at the fort.

"You reckon anybody inside there survived that?" asked Copeland.

As if in answer to his question, three gunshots rang out from the fort.

"Someone's alive in there," said Tolbert. "Keep your cover. This thing ain't over yet."

Inside the wrecked cabin, Ned Christie huddled against the front wall. The two Archies were pressed back against the far side wall. The entire wall where the blast had been set was gone. The loft was hanging down precariously. Fire was spreading. Ned could see that the whole place would soon be in flames.

"Boys," he said, "come here to me."

The two Archies ran over to join Ned Christie.

"Stay back," he said, pushing them back against the wall there beside himself. "Now, listen to me. I want you two to get out the back door. They're all around us, but I think they'll be watching this side here closest. It's still dark. Get out the back door. Stay low and move fast. Run for the woods. Try to avoid those men. Just get away. That's all."

"What about you?" said Arch Christie.

"I'll go out after you," he said. "You just do what I say now. Go find your mother. And you, Archie, you go home."

Ned watched while the two Archies opened the back door. Arch Christie looked back one last time. Ned gave him a nod, and the boys vanished from his sight through the doorway. As soon as they had stepped out, Ned began firing his Winchester. Gunfire was returned from the woods. It was concentrated on him there at the corner of the front wall and the wall that used to be. That was what he wanted. That would give the two Archies a better chance at getting to the woods undetected. He continued firing and drawing fire until the Winchester was empty. He tossed it aside. They had had enough

time anyway, he thought. He pulled out the two Colt
revolvers, one in each hand, and he cocked them. He
took a deep breath, and then he ran.

He ran through the hole the deputies had blown
in the side of his house. He ran toward the woods
firing the pistols. He ran in the same direction the
wooden shield had gone just before the blast. He ran
toward the place at the edge of the woods where he
thought the leaders of the posse would be. He ran,
and he fired as he ran, first one gun, then the other.
He ran past his shop. Wes Bowman, down on one
knee there behind the shop, turned with his revolver
in hand just as Ned ran by. He fired one shot, sending a bullet into the back of Ned Christie's head,
causing him to run forward, stumbling, a couple
more steps, then sprawl headlong in the dirt.

Lawmen came out of the woods from all directions. The first to reach the body was Dave Rusk.
With his foot he rolled it over on its back. Sam Maples came running, his eyes wild with anticipation,
his father's revolver in his hand.

"Is it Ned Christie?" he shouted.

"It's him, all right," said Rusk.

Maples stopped a few feet from the body and
stared. Then he raised the revolver and fired. He
pulled back the hammer and fired again. Paden Tolbert ran toward the scene, but by the time he had
arrived, Maples had emptied the gun. He had fired
five shots into the already lifeless body there on the
ground. Tolbert started to say something, to chastise
young Maples, but he decided it wasn't worth the

trouble. What good would it do? It was all over anyway.

"Some of you boys check the house," he said. "Be careful."

He looked up into the sky. It was clear and the moon and stars were bright.

"Yeah," he said. "Real soon now it's going to get cold."

Before the fire had reached the back wall, they took the back door off of its hinges. They laid Ned Christie's body on the door and strapped it down. Then they loaded it into the wagon. Just as they were ready to move out, to begin their return trip to Fort Smith, Watt Christie walked over to the wagon. Paden Tolbert was sitting on his horse nearby.

"I want to bury my boy," said Watt.

"I'm sorry Mr. Christie," said Tolbert, "but he has to go back with us. You can claim the body at Fort Smith. I'm sorry, but that's the way it has to be. Let's go."

Tolbert started riding. The other deputies fell in line. The wagon brought up the rear. Watt Christie stood there in silence watching the procession leave. From the crowd of onlookers nearby, Gatey stepped out and moved over by his side. Soon they were joined by Arch Christie and Young Archie Wolf who had made their way through the woods and joined the crowd. They stood there together until the wagon had rolled out of sight.

———

Their job done, the posse began breaking apart almost immediately. By the time they had reached Fayetteville, Arkansas, there were only ten of them left together. These ten, with their wagon, rode to the railroad depot. There, while Paden Tolbert was busy inside arranging their passage on to Fort Smith, a large crowd gathered outside to view the remains of the man who had been characterized to them as the worst outlaw the Indian Territory had ever seen. Photographers brought their cameras, and they propped up the heavy door that held the body of Ned Christie in order to better photograph it. They folded its arms up in order to cradle in them a Winchester rifle, and they wired them in place. Photographs were made of the body alone and of members of the posse huddled around it, holding their own weapons and looking smug, some with smiles on their faces. Different members of the posse told their versions of the battle to different reporters.

Having completely satisfied themselves that Ned Christie was indeed dead, and having gotten all the publicity they wanted out of the body, the authorities at Fort Smith allowed Watt Christie to take it home. He made the trip as quickly and directly as he could, and then, with the help of Arch Christie, Spade, and a few others, accomplished the burial. Young Archie Wolf was not there, for someone had identified him to the federal authorities as one of the men who had been with Ned Christie during the final battle, and he had fled. With the actual interment over and done, Watt and the other men who had handled the body went into the traditional three-day period of purification. Their days were spent in the sweat house, singing, fasting, sweating, praying, and drinking the purifying black drink. They emerged only at night under the masculine light of the moon. At last purified, they returned to the stomp ground for the renewing cycle of songs, dances, and prayers. And Watt Christie placed a monument over the grave of his son.

Marshal Yoes stood in front of Judge Parker's desk. Parker reached out and handed him some papers.

"What's this, Mr. Yoes?" he said.

Yoes glanced at the papers.

"It's the arrest report on Archie Wolf," he said.

"I can read," said Parker. "I don't know Archie Wolf. I don't want to know Archie Wolf."

"He was with Ned Christie," said Yoes. "He—"

"Mr. Yoes," interrupted the judge, "Ned Christie was accused of the murder of deputy Marshal Maples well over four years ago now. He was never tried, and the charges were, therefore, never proved. It took over four years for us to get Ned Christie, and then it took a twenty-three-man posse with a forty-pound cannon and six sticks of dynamite. The man was attacked by a small army and killed in his own home. The only way we can maintain our reputation, a reputation we have worked very hard to achieve, is by keeping alive the legend we have built around Ned Christie. He was a desperate man. He was the worst outlaw we have ever been confronted with. Do you understand me, Mr. Yoes?"

"Yes, sir," said Yoes. "I believe so."

"Then I suppose," the judge continued, "that you can imagine the devastating effects a trial of Mr. Wolf, or anyone else connected with Ned Christie, might have on us at this time."

"Sir?" said Yoes.

"Suppose that we were unable to substantiate in a court of law that all or any of the atrocities attributed to Ned Christie were actually perpetrated by him. Can you see the effect that would have on this court?"

"Yes, sir," said Yoes. "I think that I get your meaning."

"The whole Ned Christie case was badly handled," said the judge. "It was allowed to get way out of hand. Now I'm going to assume that this report was never filed."

He handed the papers that Yoes had dropped on the desk back to the marshal. Yoes took them.

"If you have a young man in jail," said Parker, "on whom there is no paperwork, I suggest that you turn him loose and send him on his way. Ned Christie is dead and buried. Mr. Yoes, and his monstrous legend is alive. Let's leave it that way."

Epilogue

Sam Maples was like a man haunted, possessed. With the sound of the first shot from the shadows of the woods on that fateful day just north of Tahlequah, that day that seemed at once so long ago and yet so near, with the sound of that shot Sam Maples's life had changed utterly. He had not laughed, had not even smiled since that day. In the daylight hours he walked about like a man in a trance, his expression somber and gray, his eyes glazed. At night he slept fitfully, if at all. His sleep, if sleep it was, was troubled by the same series of stark images played over and again inside his head: He heard the shots. He ran splashing into the cold water, screaming and crying. He held his father's wet, torn, and bleeding body close to him. He struggled to drag the dead weight out of the cold stream. He stood in the strange room among strangers and watched and waited as the life slowly but certainly, like a long, languid, painful exhalation, left his father's helpless, useless flesh. He saw the explosion, and he saw the shadowy figure rush toward him through the smoke and flames. He heard the shot and watched the figure fall, and he rushed toward it there on the ground.

"Is it Ned Christie?" he shouted.

And he fired his revolver over and over again into the lifeless, hated form.

This was Sam Maples's life. Would it never end?

He counted his money, and he went to the railroad station where he purchased a one-way ticket to California. It was as far from home as a train would take him, but as fast as the train carried him west, Sam kept sensing the shadows just behind him. He sometimes felt them breathing on his neck. At the far western edge of the United States they were still with him. He had not escaped. He decided to go north. He rode a steamboat up the coast and disembarked in Canada. Perhaps he thought the ghosts would not follow him across an international border. But they did.

He found work on a ranch, and in his first hard northern winter, he was alone in a line shack on a flat and desolate prairie, alone with Canadian cattle and the Ozark ghosts. He had ridden twelve miles to a trading post to buy a few supplies for the shack: some coffee, beans, tobacco. While the trader wrapped up his purchases, Sam counted out his change on the counter.

"You got far to go, young fellow?" asked the trader.

"Line shack about twelve miles out," said Sam.

"Well," said the trader, "don't dawdle. Big

storm's a brewing. I'd hurry on home if I was you. Either that or find a place around here to stay the night."

Sam left and rode for the line shack. He did not want the company of men. He had gone about six miles when the storm struck. It seemed to come all at once. It was biting cold and blinding. The cold snow seemed to blow right through his body. He pulled his hat down low and ducked his head, and soon, he realized that he no longer had any sense of direction. He was lost in a vicious swirl of ice and snow. Everything was white, blinding white. He hurt with the cold, and his soul was frozen with the fear of it. It was alive, and it was malicious, and it knew him by name.

Then he realized that he was sitting on the ground. He couldn't remember falling off his horse or dismounting. He didn't know where the animal had gone. He couldn't move, but he no longer felt the cold or pain. He felt nothing. He was numb. He slowly drifted into calm oblivion.

Coda

Ned Christie
  Born Dec. 14, 1852
  Died Nov. 3, 1892
  He was at one time a member of
  the Executive Council of the C.N.
  He was a blacksmith and a brave man.

Author's Note

Ned Christie's War is a novel. Based on history and intended to reflect the character of its leading players and the spirit of the times, it is not intended to be specific and accurate in all details. It is a work of fiction, and it includes some fictitious characters. In some cases, historical figures have been consolidated into one character. Readers who are looking for detailed and documented history are urged to consult *The Last Cherokee Warriors* by Phillip Steele (Pelican Pub. Co., Gretna, Louisiana, 1974) and *The Killing of Ned Christie: Cherokee Outlaw* by Bonnie Stahlman Speer (Reliance Press, Norman, Oklahoma, 1990) for not only well researched but readable nonfiction accounts of the Ned Christie story.

ROBERT J. CONLEY
TAHLEQUAH
THE CHEROKEE NATION